"Sullivan, I Understand Why You Don't Want Me Back In Denver.

"You were angry with me for leaving. You thought I was selfish and ambitious and perhaps you were right—"

"Nothing's wrong with ambition," he interrupted. "You stepped on me to climb the ladder. Well, if I was fool enough to let a nineteen-year-old kid dump on me, too bad."

"It wasn't like that."

"It was exactly like that. I gave you a job. You had talent and looks. Nothing wrong there. But I let you get under my skin. You were a kid, and I wanted you."

"Sullivan." Kay reached out, but he pulled back.

"No. I don't want you touching me again. Can't we call it even? I broke the rules, but so did you. You left without so much as a good-bye."

Near tears, Kay said, "Oh, Sul, I didn't want to, but you—" She broke off, knowing nothing she said now could repair the hurt she'd caused.

Dear Reader,

Welcome to Silhouette! Our goal is to give you hours of unbeatable reading pleasure, and we hope you'll enjoy each month's six new Silhouette Desires. These sensual, provocative love stories are both believable and compelling—sometimes they're poignant, sometimes humorous, but always enjoyable.

Indulge yourself. Experience all the passion and excitement of falling in love along with our heroine as she meets the irresistible man of her dreams and together they overcome all obstacles in the path to a happy ending.

If this is your first Desire, I hope it'll be the first of many. If you're already a Silhouette Desire reader, thanks for your support! Look for some of your favorite authors in the coming months: Stephanie James, Diana Palmer, Dixie Browning, Ann Major and Doreen Owens Malek, to name just a few.

Happy reading!

Isabel Swift
Senior Editor

SDRL-7/85

NAN RYAN
Love in the Air

Silhouette Desire

Published by Silhouette Books New York

America's Publisher of Contemporary Romance

SILHOUETTE BOOKS
300 East 42nd St., New York, N.Y. 10017

Copyright © 1986 by Nancy Henderson Ryan

ISBN: 0-373-05351-7

First Silhouette Books printing May 1987
Second printing May 1987

America's Publisher of Contemporary Romance

Printed in the U.S.A.

NAN RYAN,

born and raised in Texas, has lived literally from "one border of the United States to the other" and lots of places in between. Seattle, San Diego, El Paso, Dallas, Houston, Albuquerque, Denver and Mobile are some of the cities she's called home. Currently she lives with her husband, Joe, in a suburb of Atlanta, Georgia, where she writes in her cluttered sun-room office and co-hosts *Atlanta Book Ends*, a biweekly book review program on WVEU television. Her first published work, a Civil War novel entitled *Kathleen's Surrender*, was well received by the critics. In June '87 Worldwide Library will publish her second historical, *Desert Storm*.

For My Sister, Judy Jonas.
More Precious Now Than Ever.

One

Kay Clark, smiling at the tall, uniformed driver holding the door open, stepped into the back seat of the long, sleek limousine. She sighed contentedly, crossed her legs and settled back against the plush gray upholstery, grateful that the thoughtful chauffeur had left the motor running. The air-conditioned interior of the big limo was a welcome sanctuary to the tired young woman.

The neat, uniformed man had met her at the outermost gate of Stapleton International Airport and briefly explained that Sam Shults was unable to meet her, but that a car had been sent to take her to her hotel in downtown Denver. She had nodded, handed her carryon luggage to him and let him effectively guide her through the throngs of Labor Day travelers rushing into and out of the massive airport.

The hot, dry air that whooshed up to meet them the moment they stepped out onto the sidewalk was a jolt, even though Kay had been reading about the long, record-breaking hot spell that crossed the state of Colorado. It had been drizzling rain and no more than seventy degrees when she'd arrived at LAX in Los Angeles only a couple of hours ago. Foolishly, she'd dressed for the west-coast weather instead of the sweltering Denver September.

Leaning up a bit on the soft cushion, Kay shrugged out of the long-sleeved navy, heat-attracting blazer, dropped it across her lap and raised both hands to rake them through the wilted, silvery hair clinging to her neck. The uniformed chauffeur, having loaded her luggage into the limo's trunk, slid into the driver's seat, turned to look at her over his shoulder and said apologetically, "I'm sorry the weather is so warm. I'm sure it must seem unbearable to you, coming from Los Angeles."

"It is hot," Kay admitted and smiled. "But then, Denver's my home, so I'm not that surprised. I've seen it this hot before in early September."

"I see." He nodded into the rearview mirror, shifted into drive and maneuvered the long, sleek car out into the never-ending stream of airport traffic.

Kay was glad he made no further attempt at conversation. She wanted only to silently observe the dear, familiar surroundings of the breathtakingly beautiful city she thought of as home. As though the quiet, dignified driver could look into her thoughts, he bypassed the quicker, shorter route into downtown, heading instead out Colorado Boulevard and turning onto the winding Cherry Creek Drive, one of the loveliest streets in the city, its wide median manicured and heavy with verdant foliage and ancient, towering trees.

Smiling foolishly, Kay twisted around, taking in the sights and finally lifting her eyes to the majestic Rockies, reaching to the sky on the western horizon. Hot though it was in Denver proper, snow dusted the highest peaks. The huge, fiery Indian-summer sun was beginning to slip below those white-capped mountains.

The big car purred to a stop directly in front of the stately old Brown Palace Hotel. Kay felt her heart constrict. She'd spent the night in this famous inn only once in her life. As she walked into the imposing, multitiered lobby, she was, as she had been before, impressed by the design and magnificence of a structure built so long ago. Her eyes automatically lifted to the wraparound balcony at the fifth-floor level. Midway down the east wall, the door to room 503 pulled at her.

Kay whirled around, stepped up to the smiling desk clerk and announced in a weak voice, "I'm Ms. Kay Clark. I'm to—"

"Yes, indeed." The short, bespectacled man beamed at her. "I remember you. You were on Q102 radio with Sullivan Ward."

"You're right and I—"

"Yes, yes." He smiled knowingly. "Sam Shults has been calling to see if you've checked in. Welcome back to Denver and to the Brown Palace." He snapped his fingers and a young blond bellman hurried toward them.

"Thank you, it's good to be back," Kay responded.

"Good to have you home. Everyone's excited about you being back on the air with Sullivan Ward." He handed a key to the beaming bellman. "Take the lady to 503."

"No, I... have you another... that is..."

"Is something wrong, Miss Clark?" The desk clerk's bushy brows were knitted together. "Mr. Shults asked that we give you one of our nicest rooms and so I—"

"Room 503 is fine. Just fine," Kay managed. She turned and followed the tall blond youth loaded down with her gray suede luggage.

"Will there be anything else, ma'am?" The young man's face reddened when he backed away toward the door after he'd carefully placed all of Kay's suitcases in the dressing area.

"Nothing more." Kay grinned up at him and handed him his tip.

"You need anything, you just ask for Ron." He stuffed the bills into his pocket and disappeared.

Kay locked the door behind him and stood looking dumbly at the heavy mahogany, reluctant to turn around. She took a deep breath, slowly turned and finally let her eyes stray across the spacious, high-ceilinged room to the big,

king-size bed. The massive bed was in exactly the same place
it had been on that night five years before. Kay could vividly recall that the sheets were ice-blue on that other occasion.

Hurriedly, she crossed the room, furiously jerked at the
silky, down-filled comforter and peeled it to the foot of the
bed. She moaned. Soft, clean sheets of ice blue looked cool
and oh-so-inviting. Upon that big, blue bed, Kay could see
again a long, lean body, unclothed and masculinely beautiful, stretched out in peaceful slumber. Handsome face in
repose, ebony hair disheveled. Broad, hair-matted chest
rising and falling evenly. Hard abdomen and narrow hips;
long, powerful legs dusted with coal-black hair.

She'd left him like that on that morning five years ago.
She'd tiptoed out of the room without waking him. A sad
little smile lifted the corners of Kay's mouth. In all the times
she'd thought of him since, she always pictured him gloriously naked in this blue bed. He'd looked so vulnerable,
so innocent, so unashamed, lying there sleeping, uncov-
ered.

Kay slowly slid a hand over the cool, silky blue sheets and
stood up. A huge bouquet of long-stemmed Happiness roses
drew her attention to the massive mahogany dresser opposite the bed. Stepping up to the tall bureau, she leaned to
smell one of the velvety flowers, drawing the card from beneath a satin bow.

It said: "Sorry I couldn't meet the plane; was tied up. Will
make it up to you. The wife and I, along with Sullivan
Ward, want to take you out to dinner tonight. Will call for
you at 8:30 this evening. Welcome back!" It was signed
"Sam Shults."

Kay lowered the card. And she began to tremble. In exactly one hour she would see Sullivan Ward again after five
years.

Sullivan Ward stepped from his shower, toweled his tall,
wet body, knotted a dry towel atop his left hip and reached
for a cigarette. Barefoot, he padded into the pine-paneled
den and went behind the bar. From a mirrored shelf he took

down a carved crystal decanter of Scotch. He poured a tiny portion into a cocktail glass, added soda, a twist of lemon and a couple of ice cubes then circled the bar.

Sullivan walked directly to the two-story window forming the entire front wall of the big room. Squinting, he looked into the dying rays of the setting sun rapidly slipping below the mountain peaks. He took a swallow of his Scotch, made a face and set the drink on a handy glass-topped table. He sighed heavily.

Damn her anyway. Damn Kay Clark. She'd ripped his guts out five years ago and now she was back. Back to live in Denver. Back to take her old job at the radio station. Back to open up old wounds that had finally healed. Uh-uh, lady, he thought. No way. Not this time.

Sullivan ran a lean brown hand through his ebony hair, padded into the bedroom and began dressing for dinner. He'd be at the restaurant to welcome his old morning-show partner back to town, just as though he was delighted she'd returned. If Sammy Shults wanted her on the air with him, well, Sam was the boss. Hadn't he tried to tell Sam that Kay Clark wanted to return only because she couldn't cut it in L.A. radio? No matter, the ambitious little heartbreaker was here again to do her time in the minor leagues until she could find herself a better deal.

Sullivan buttoned his white shirt and pulled on the trousers to a dark suit. Well, maybe they'd both get lucky and she'd get an offer by Christmas and get her cute rear end out of Denver. Sullivan dropped onto his bed to put on dark socks and black leather shoes. Then, too, perhaps her rear was no longer as cute as before. Maybe she'd had one sausage pizza too many—she never could resist them—and she'd grown as broad as she was tall. Maybe that long silvery hair she used to toss in his face had been chopped off short and had turned yellow.

Sullivan rose from the bed, slid a maroon silk tie beneath the stiff turned-up collar of his shirt and tied it in a perfect knot. He pulled his suit jacket from its wooden hanger and walked into the den once again. He cast a quick look at the shiny gold watch nestled in the dark hair of his wrist. It was eight o'clock.

Sullivan Ward trembled.

Kay, an air of cool confidence belying her true feelings, swept into the Turn of the Century restaurant on the fatherly arm of a jovial, affectionate Sam Shults, the general manager of radio station Q102. On Sam's other arm, his pleasantly plump, warmhearted wife, Betty Jane, was as happy as her husband to have Kay Clark back.

The laughing, chattering trio was escorted through the main room of the busy east Denver eatery and up a half-flight of stairs into the cheerful garden court. It was a small, intimate room with a few round, white linen-draped tables and half a dozen red-leather banquettes. Green plants filled every spare inch of floor space and cascaded downward from the high ceiling, making it necessary for very tall men to occasionally bend to pass beneath the leafy canopy.

A well-groomed, willowy lady in a long black dress led the threesome to a choice banquette, its strategic location offering a panoramic view of the Front Range through spotless floor-to-ceiling glass.

"Honey, you slide in there." Sam Shults took Kay's elbow. "I'll sit here by mama, and when Sullivan arrives, he'll keep you company."

"That'll be fine," Kay said pleasantly, her stomach jerking at the mere thought of the imposing, magnetic Sullivan seated in the booth close beside her.

"Kay, I swear you're just prettier than ever." Betty Shults was beaming across the table at her. "I'll bet when Sullivan sees you tonight, that permanent scowl he's worn lately will disappear."

Sam Shults shot his wife a sidelong, silencing glance. "Now, sugar," he gently scolded, "you shouldn't be—"

"Samuel John Shults, don't be telling me what I should and should not do." Betty smiled at her husband and Sam gave a little sigh of resignation.

"Pay Betty no mind, Kay," Sam said. "You know how she is about Sullivan. Lordy, you'd think she'd borne him.

She sees the least little expression of displeasure on his face and she immediately—"

"Is Sullivan very unhappy about my coming back?"

"Why, Kay, how could you think such a thing? You know he—"

Betty Shults interrupted her stammering husband. "Kay, you know that I always speak my mind. Sullivan wasn't too thrilled when Sam told him you'd be coming back to be his morning-show partner. In fact, he said—"

"Damn it, Betty, who runs the station, me or you?" An obviously uncomfortable Sam summoned a waiter, and looked relieved when the slim mustard-jacketed man hurried to take their drink order. "Kay, what will you have?"

"Just a glass of white wine," Kay managed weakly. Betty Shults, after telling her husband she'd like a piña colada, again was talking, but to Kay's relief, she'd changed the subject.

"Then last year we built a new pool, with a redwood deck and a hot tub, on that rise out behind the house. You must come out for the weekend." Betty continued, but Kay, nodding absently now and then, found it impossible to be terribly interested in the many home improvements at the Shults estate. Sipping slowly at her wine, Kay silently begged her tensed muscles to relax. Why should Betty's revelation regarding Sullivan's reaction to her return be shocking? She'd hardly expected him to be overjoyed with the news. Indeed, she'd prepared herself mentally to absorb a certain amount of verbal abuse from him. Sullivan could be cold and ruthless. He could be downright nasty when something or someone displeased him.

Kay gritted her teeth. She could take what he dished out. She was no longer a nineteen-year-old kid to be bossed around by him. He'd almost totally controlled her from the moment he gave her the much-coveted job as his partner on the morning show. She'd been only seventeen years old then, and everyone was more than a little shocked when he'd chosen an inexperienced teenager to be with him on the air.

Sullivan paid no attention to the gossip and told her not to concern herself with it. She'd sent in an audition tape just

like all the other hopefuls. Sullivan had patiently listened to
each and every one and when he'd played hers, something
in her voice intrigued and impressed him. He had no idea,
he assured her and his boss, Sam Shults, that the melodious, confident voice on the tape belonged to a seventeen-
year-old who had no broadcasting experience.

Impressed by what he'd heard, Sullivan called Kay Clark
and asked her to come in for an interview. She could still
recall the startled look on his handsome face when she shyly
entered his office. Quickly regaining his cool composure, he
smiled warmly, offered her a chair and went about letting
her down as painlessly as possible.

"Sweetheart," he'd said very softly, "let me first say to
you that you have a lovely voice and a lot of talent, but—"

"But what, Mr. Ward?" she'd brashly cut in.

"Honey, you're a little young to be working anywhere,
don't you think? You should be in school." His dark,
flashing eyes held a slightly bemused look that annoyed Kay.
"How old are you, Kay?"

Kay lifted her small chin. "I'll be eighteen on my next
birthday, Mr. Ward, and as for school, I graduated from
high school a year ago and I'm a part-time student at the
University of Denver." He was still smiling and he threw
back his head and laughed aloud when she said, "Just how
old are you, Mr. Sullivan Ward?"

"I'll be thirty my next birthday, Kay, so as you can see,
the age difference between us—"

"Has nothing whatsoever to do with what I came here for
this morning. I sent in an audition tape; you listened and
you liked it. Now I deserve the promised opportunity to cut
a demo tape with you and you've no right to back out on me
simply because I'm not . . ."

"Okay, okay." He lifted his hands in the air, palms out.
"You win, Kay Clark." Grinning, he'd circled his big desk,
pulled her to her feet and guided her down the hall to the
production studio. "Let's go cut that tape, honey. I can see
you're a mighty determined young lady."

"Is that so bad?" Kay had tilted her blond head to look
up at the towering man leading her down the hall.

Sullivan Ward looked down into her young, upturned face, shook his dark head and admitted, "I hope not, because I'm the same way."

"Well, will you come, Kay?" Betty Shults's slightly shrill voice pulled Kay back to the present.

"I . . . I'm sorry, Betty. What did you say?"

"Are you all right, Kay? You seem a million miles away." Betty patted at her short chestnut hair, took a sip of her sweet pineapple drink and stared at Kay.

"I'm just fine, really," Kay apologized. "Now what did you ask me?" She smiled engagingly and vowed she'd keep her mind on what her table companions were saying.

"I just suggested that you come out to the house on Sunday. We could charcoal some steaks and swim in the pool."

"For goodness' sakes, Betty, she just got off the plane," Sam Shults intervened. "Give her a chance, will you? She's got to hunt for an apartment, have meetings at the station and . . . I wonder what's keeping Sullivan. I'm starving and I'll bet you are, too, Kay."

Feeling as though she never wanted to eat again, Kay said, "A little, yes." Her eyes once again darted toward the room's entrance. It was past time for Sullivan's arrival. Any second now he'd walk through that door, duck his head to pass beneath the low-hanging plants and come toward her. Kay took a hurried gulp of wine as her heart tried to pound its way out of her chest.

"Mr. Shults." A tall tuxedoed man, manager of the restaurant, stepped up to the banquette. "Sorry to disturb you." He nodded graciously to the ladies. "You've a telephone call."

Kay knew.

She knew who was calling Sam Shults at the Turn of the Century. Cold fingers curled tightly around the fluted wineglass, she smiled calmly when Sam Shults returned, looking sheepish and embarrassed.

"That was Sullivan on the phone." He glanced first at Kay, then at his wife. "He can't make it this evening. He's terribly sorry, but it seems . . ."

Kay never heard the rest of the explanation. Sullivan wasn't coming. He wasn't coming because he did not want to see her. She was both relieved and disappointed.

This was going to be harder than she thought.

Sullivan Ward slowly replaced the receiver, set the phone aside and frantically tore at the perfect knot in his silk tie. He shrugged out of his expensive suit coat, wadded it up as though it were a shapeless sweatshirt and threw it across the room. It fluttered down the pine-covered wall into a dark, discarded heap on the gray carpet. The maroon tie followed the jacket.

Jaw set, eyes cold, Sullivan jerked furiously at the buttons of his white dress shirt, sending a couple of the small pearly disks flying. He lifted the toe of his left shoe to the heel of his right, pushing it from his foot. He repeated the action on the other. From the glass-topped table he took a half empty package of cigarettes and a gold lighter. He jammed a cigarette between tight lips, flicked the lighter and inhaled. Slowly he lowered the slim lighter and stared at the shiny gold. A thumb idly rubbed back and forth over the small script on the lighter's smooth surface. "SUL" was all it said. No one but Kay Clark had ever been allowed to call him that.

The tiny gold lighter was hurled after the coat and tie. When it hit the pine wall, it made a resounding thud that sounded like a minor explosion in the quiet, twilight-bathed room.

Sullivan Ward felt the explosion in his aching heart.

Feelings bruised by Sullivan's obvious desire to put off their imminent reunion for as long as possible, Kay said breezily, "I'm just as glad Sullivan can't make it, gives me the chance to visit with you two." She smiled warmly at a frowning, flustered Sam Shults.

Lips pursed, a hint of satisfaction in her tone, Betty Shults looked accusingly at her displeased husband. "I told you he wouldn't show up, Sam. I knew darned well he'd—"

"Betty, Sullivan didn't come because something unexpected came up and—"

"Oh, sure," she said flippantly, "the president and the first lady dropped by for drinks just as he was walking out the door." She smiled at Kay. "Or his closet caught fire and he could find nothing to wear."

"That's enough." Sam gave her a scathing look. "Let's eat."

The food at the Turn of the Century had always been superb, but tonight Kay had to struggle to eat enough to keep from arousing the suspicion of the two hearty eaters seated across from her. While the Shultses successfully dismissed the absent Sullivan from their minds, it was not so easy for Kay. Telling herself that perhaps he did have some unavoidable business, she knew, deep down, that he decided at the last minute not to join them because he dreaded seeing her again.

Kay felt relieved when the evening was finally over and the Shultses had dropped her back at the Brown Palace, and sighed when she stepped inside the suite and locked the door. Feeling weary and wilted, Kay kicked off her shoes and eagerly unzipped her silk dress, letting it slide down her arms and over her hips. In seconds she'd completely stripped and stood under a pelting shower, eyes closed, face turned up to the pounding spray.

Yawning, Kay toweled herself dry, slipped on a pair of eggshell crepe pajamas, sat down on the edge of the turned-down bed and stretched her arms lazily in the air. Certain she was so exhausted from the long, tiring day that she would fall immediately asleep, Kay switched off the lamp on the bedside table and crawled in between the cool, ice-blue sheets.

She'd left the drapes at the window across the room open. Only transparent sheers of filmy white covered the tall plate glass. The big, cool suite was suffused with soft light streaming from the tall downtown skyscrapers and into the quiet privacy of this fifth-floor room. Everything in the well-appointed suite took on a soft, ethereal form.

Kay, alone in the big blue bed, let her gaze slide slowly around the room. The scent of roses wafted to her from the big bouquet on the bureau, the fragrance but one more reminder of that other fateful night she'd spent here. Then, too, there'd been roses, dozens of roses, all sent by Sullivan Ward.

Roses and champagne and Sullivan. Tears slowly slipping down her cheeks, Kay, as she had a thousand times over the past five years, again let time turn back. She was nineteen years old and she was in this very room. Soft lights washed over the bed and the scent of roses made her dizzy. The taste of champagne was on the heated lips that kept kissing her. A deep male voice, its timbre caressing, persuasive, had murmured passionate words into her ear. Warm, sure hands had glided tenderly over her trembling flesh.

It had been her last night in Denver. She was to depart very early the next morning for Los Angeles and the new position at one of the top radio stations there. Sullivan had taken her out to dinner on that last evening, a night of dry August heat and bright moonlight. She'd worn a cool cotton sundress, its sheered bodice hugging her braless curves, narrow straps going over her tanned shoulders to tie in a bow at the back of her neck. Her almost waist-length hair had been pulled into a casual shiny twist and pinned atop her head.

Sullivan, boyishly handsome in a white knit shirt straining across his chest and faded jeans, had honored her wish to dine on sausage pizza at a little Italian place up in the foothills of west Denver. They'd laughed throughout the meal, joking and teasing one another, both cautiously avoiding the subject of Kay's impending move.

Long before midnight, Sullivan, knowing she had to catch an early flight, agreed they should call it a night. Holding hands and growing increasingly silent, they exited from the creaking elevator on the fifth floor of the Brown and went to room 503. Sullivan unlocked the door, motioned Kay inside and followed her.

When she reached out to flip on the lights, Sullivan's hand stopped her. His dark, sultry eyes on her mouth, he slowly pulled her fingers to his chest and said simply, "Kay."

When his dark, handsome head descended slowly to her, Kay tilted hers back and her mouth eagerly parted to receive his kiss. Gentle, sculpted lips settled on hers, warm and undemanding. With his mouth covering hers, Sullivan again whispered, "Kay, oh, my Kay."

Kay sighed as his kiss became more demanding, filling her with warmth, just as it always did. Her arms went up around his neck, her fingers anxiously twisting at the black, thick hair curling over the collar of his clean knit shirt.

She loved kissing Sullivan. His kisses set her afire; they had from the first time he'd unexpectedly kissed her one frigid winter morning. She had hurried into the control room, her nose red, her eyes smarting, her teeth chattering. He'd looked up at her, grinned, rose and came to her. Wordlessly he'd taken her in his arms, held her for a minute, put a thumb beneath her quivering chin and bent to her, his lips covering her cold ones in a rapidly heating kiss.

Since that cold, snowy morning, he'd kissed her often and she never failed to respond and glory in the feel of his mouth upon hers. More than once their hunger for each other had made kissing, no matter how wonderful, seem inadequate. Still, Sullivan, though his eyes had looked tortured and his body had trembled with his need, had many times thrust her away from him, stopping short of what they both wanted. Needed.

Not tonight.

Now he was kissing her with unbridled passion and she met his hunger with her own. When their heated lips separated for breath, Sullivan, his broad chest rising and falling rapidly, urged Kay toward the bed. She willingly took a seat on its edge and watched as he pulled off his shirt. He stood looking down at her and Kay's eyes admiringly swept over the wide smooth shoulders and the hard, muscled chest covered with a mat of crisp, black hair that gradually narrowed to a thick line down his hard abdomen.

Sullivan took a seat beside her, a long arm going around her shoulders. "Sweetheart," he said huskily, as a big hand moved up to the swell of her breasts, "it's our last night. Kiss me like it's the last night, honey. Kiss me, baby."

"Sul," she murmured and put her palms to his smoothly shaven cheeks. Her soft, moist mouth, aggressively open, came up to his. She slowly ran the tip of her tongue inside his upper lip, just the way he'd taught her to do. He groaned and pulled her to him. Their mouths melded and while they hungrily kissed, Kay could feel the crinkly hair of Sullivan's warm chest pleasantly tickling the rise of her breasts above the bodice of her sundress. She softly moaned as her nipples hardened and her breasts swelled. Instinctively, she pressed closer to the heat and hardness of that masculine chest.

At last Sullivan's mouth left hers, trailing fiery kisses across her flushed cheek and finally coming to rest on her ear. "Kay, I want to feel your breasts against me. Just for a minute, sweetheart, just for a while," he said.

Before she could answer, his mouth took hers again, his tongue thrusting between her parted lips to mate with hers. Deft fingers untied the bow at her nape and gentle, caring hands peeled down the white cotton barrier from between them as his lips left hers. He looked unwaveringly into her eyes while the dress—along with her inhibitions—was lowered.

Unhampered by clothes, Kay's full, high breasts rose and fell with her rapid, nervous breaths, and her bottom lip trembled as she lowered her eyes from his. "Sul," she began raggedly.

"Sweetheart," he soothed softly, lean hands rising to cup the soft, warm mounds of creamy flesh. "You're so very beautiful. Don't be embarrassed with me, Kay. Look at me, darling."

Slowly her eyes lifted to his. While his thumbs teased at the rose-hued crests, she sighed softly and shyly admitted, "That feels good, Sul. So good."

"My sweet baby," he murmured and slowly, gently pulled her against him. "Put your arms around me," he in-

structed as his hands spread lightly on her back, pressing her
tenderly to him.

Kay's slender arms clasped him tightly as she gloried in
the exquisite delight of Sullivan's warm, hair-roughened
chest touching her aching, swelling breasts. Automatically
arching her back to press closer, she sighed and turned her
face into his brown throat, inhaling deeply of his clean,
masculine scent. While every part of her body glowed with
delicious rising heat, Sullivan cradled her head in his hand
and again took her mouth with his own.

In his kiss was all his love, all his passion, all his hunger.
Kay reeled with the intensity of emotions he'd unleashed in
her as well as himself. His kiss was hungry, demanding,
devastating, and when their lips and tongues finally separated, his breath was labored, his bare chest heaving, his
sultry eyes almost wild. Decisively, he pushed her slowly
down across the bed, following her. Kay could feel the soft
fabric of the bedspread beneath her naked back. Sullivan's
hard, handsome face was looking down at her. His weight
supported on an elbow, he was leaning over her and saying
things he'd never said to her before.

"My God," he mused honestly, "have you any idea how
long I've wanted to see you like this, to look at you?" A
hand was at her breast, gently caressing, a thumb circling
the hard peak.

"Sul," she whispered, her fingers happily exploring the
hard muscled chest above her, "I've wanted this, too,
I've—"

Her sentence wasn't finished. His lips were on hers again,
nibbling, playing, tasting, while his broad chest pressed
heavily down on her naked breasts. Kay's hands were in the
thick, dark hair of his head while her open mouth twisted
under his and her tingling torso rubbed unashamedly on
him. When a hand slipped from Kay's narrow waist and
down over the folds of her white cotton skirt, Kay made no
move to stop him. Nor did she protest when that hand slid
underneath her skirt and moved with slow determination up
a smooth thigh.

Kay wasn't quite certain how or when those practiced, persuasive hands managed to divest her of her lacy panties, but she fleetingly recalled them slipping over her hips, down her legs and fluttering through the air.

It was the last time she thought of her panties.

That warm male hand was again moving up a trembling thigh and a deep, drugging voice so familiarly dear was murmuring close to her face, "I have to touch you, Kay. I have to, honey. I won't hurt you, I'd never hurt you."

"Yes," was all she could manage, as those long, lean fingers moved unerringly to that sensitive feminine flesh where no man's hands had ever been before. "Yes, yes," she whispered through fevered lips, her blue eyes widening with a new and unbelievable pleasure.

His eyes upon her sweet, flushed face, Sullivan stroked her gently, coaxingly. She writhed and clung to him and looked up with eyes both frightened and happy.

"There, sweetness," he soothed softly, staying with her, tenderly caressing, patiently tutoring her, bringing her pleasure, possessively introducing her to the secrets of her beautiful body. While she tossed her head back and forth and murmured his name in wonder and fear, Sullivan continued to take her slowly. He caringly brought her toward release while the heart in his bare chest thudded with a heavy cadence and his tight jeans strained with the fullness of his aching arousal.

Finally her zenith began and Kay's blue, shining eyes widened with shocked surprise. She clung to Sullivan's bare wide shoulders so tightly her long nails cut into his flesh. He smiled down at her, his hand continuing rhythmically to stroke, his voice, deep and soft, saying lovingly, "Yes, my baby, I'm here. I won't let you go."

When she lay at last limp in Sullivan's protective arms, Kay willingly let him finish undressing her. Moments later they were both naked upon the bed that Sullivan had turned down. With half emptied glasses of champagne beside them on the bedside table, soft music coming from the radio and the scent of roses sweetening the air, they completed the act of lovemaking upon sheets of ice blue. Kay knew as Sullivan lowered his sleek, bare body onto hers that the brief pain of his penetration would pale beside the pain of leaving him.

And she was right.

Kay blinked at the tears that had begun to slide down her cheeks. How right she had been on that long-ago night to realize leaving Sullivan would cause great pain. Pain for her. Pain for him.

Still she had recklessly walked away, telling herself it was really all his fault. He hadn't asked her to stay. Hadn't told her to stay. If he had, she would have snuggled happily into his strong arms and said worshipfully, "Yes, I'll stay. I want only to be with you. I love you."

Kay threw back the silky blue sheets and got up. Sighing wearily, she walked to the window and stood staring out at the twinkling Denver lights. Lights distorted by her tear-blurred vision.

The truth was painful, but it was time she faced it.

It was her fault. Nobody else's. She had been head-over-heels in love with Sullivan Ward, but she was so young and so foolish. She had sacrificed what they had together for a glamorous, high-paying radio job in L.A. And through all these years of regretting her foolish choice, and longing for all that she had lost, she had soothed her wounded heart by telling herself it was as much Sullivan's fault as her own.

That simply was not true.

She, of her own free will, had walked out on the most magnificent man she would ever meet, sacrificing a precious once-in-a-lifetime love to chase youthful dreams of fame and glory. She was responsible for their breakup. Her career had meant more to her than Sul.

"Dear God, what a little fool I was," murmured Kay tearfully to the loneliness of the room where once she had known the ecstasy of Sullivan's arms. "If I had it all to do over again..."

Tiredly, Kay went back to the big blue bed. Exhaustion soon blessedly overtook her and in minutes she was asleep.

Two

Kay was awakened the next morning by brilliant September sunshine streaming into the room. Pushing her long, sleep-tousled hair out of her eyes, she pushed a pillow against the headboard and sat up. Sleepy blue eyes glanced to the night table beside her with its built-in radio below. Kay reached out and flipped the on button, filling the room with music. She leaned over, squinting, and smiled. The radio was tuned to Q102. Sullivan's morning show. Any second now the record would end.

"That was the old Gloria Gaynor hit 'I Will Survive.'" The deep unmistakable voice so affected Kay that she realized she was holding her breath. "Isn't that a good song?" Sullivan asked his audience, his deep melodious voice like warm, smooth honey. Kay sank back against the pillows and commanded her pulse to slow down. Closing her eyes, she leaned her head back and listened while that deep, naturally sensual voice effortlessly drew her to him, just as it did his other listeners. He was the best she'd ever heard. There'd been no one on the west coast to compare with this talented man. She'd like to tell him that when they met again, but she had a feeling Sullivan would no longer care what she thought of him.

By ten o'clock, Kay, dressed in a tailored suit of beige poplin with a wide multicolored belt adding a splash of color, walked through the glass double doors of radio station Q102, high atop the Petroleum Club building in downtown Denver. A fresh-faced young woman with hair of auburn and big green eyes looked up, smiled and said almost worshipfully, "You have to be Kay Clark!" The woman jumped up from her chair, pressing her palms to her coloring cheeks. "I'm Sherry Jones and I've heard so much about you, Ms. Clark. Why, it's like having a movie star in the station. I want your autograph; I just have to . . ."

Shaking her head, Kay laughed good-naturedly. "Sherry, I'm flattered, but I'm hardly a star. Is Mr. Shults busy?"

"Follow me, Ms. Clark." Sherry was smiling happily. "Gosh, you're so pretty. You and Sullivan will make a pair. He's so handsome, you know."

"Yes." Kay nodded. "I know."

Kay followed the friendly young woman into Sam Shults's big office. "She's here," Sherry announced to the stocky man rising from behind his heavy oak desk. "Shall I bring coffee?"

"Morning, Kay." Sam Shults came to meet her. "Kay doesn't drink coffee, Sherry."

Sherry bobbed her auburn head. Grinning, she clasped her hands in front of her, rooted to the spot, staring at Kay. "Would you like to go to lunch with me, Ms. Clark?" Sherry ventured hopefully.

"Sherry—" Sam Shults put on his gruff voice "—I see five lights blinking on the switchboard. Think you could tear yourself away to go back out to your desk and answer a few calls?"

"Oh, sorry, Mr. Shults." The impressionable young woman backed away, lifting a hand to wave goodbye to Kay. "We usually eat over at Leo's, Kay, so—"

"Sherry!" Sam Shults pointed to the door. She hunched her shoulders, winked at Kay and scooted out the door.

"Now," Sam said when he and Kay were alone, "have a seat and let's go over a few things."

"Sam," Kay said, taking the leather chair across from her old boss, "will you level with me?"

"Why, Kay, haven't I always?" He looked puzzled. Dropping back down into his padded chair, he laced his stubby fingers together atop his desk. "What's on your mind? I thought we settled on your salary."

Kay lifted a slender hand in the air. "I'm not concerned about the salary; it's plenty generous. I'm concerned about Sullivan Ward." She looked directly into Sam Shults's soft brown eyes.

His beefy shoulders slumped. "Kay, what can I tell you? We both know that—"

"Sullivan doesn't want me here. Is that it?"

Sam Shults, reluctant to meet her gaze, sighed. "Kay, Sullivan is a pro. When you're on the air together, he'll be just like he was before."

"You didn't answer my question, Sam."

"I'm the general manager of Q102. I have to decide what is best for this station without a great deal of regard to personal feelings."

Kay smiled sadly. "You just answered my question."

Sam Shults smiled with her. "I guess I did. Honey, you and Sullivan will just have to work out any personality problems. I care about one thing—audience."

"Why, Sammy, you're as sentimental as ever," Kay kidded.

"Yeah—" Sam Shults reddened "—that's what Betty tells me."

After half an hour Sam said, "That about does it, I believe. If you've nothing further to ask, I'll turn you over to Sullivan." He looked at her questioningly and rose.

Kay stood up. "Do you suppose Daniel was just a bit nervous when he was tossed into the lion's den?"

Sam grinned at her. "In this case, I've a feeling the lion is just as jittery."

* * *

He was tall and slim and graceful. His hair was shiny black except for a sprinkling of silver streaking his temples. His face looked a little leaner, harder and more handsome than ever. Lazy-lidded dark eyes were looking at her and Kay felt unaccountably warm despite the coldness of his gaze. The full male mouth was stretched into a welcoming smile that didn't extend to his eyes.

His shoulders, wider than she'd remembered, were unnaturally rigid, and his broad chest was noticeably rising and falling beneath a shirt of pale-blue cotton. Crisp, black hair curled appealingly from the open throat and upon dark forearms revealed by rolled-up sleeves. Hard-finish black trousers draped perfectly over narrow hips and closely fitted the sinewy thighs and long legs.

At thirty-six years old, Sullivan Ward was at the peak of his rugged masculine appeal. Kay stared at him in awe. And in fear. His icy, handsome face told her what she'd suspected. He didn't want her here. He was sorry she'd returned, and Kay had the uneasy feeling he planned to make her sorry, too.

Coolly assessing her, Sullivan finally nodded his dark head and said evenly, "Ms. Clark."

"Mr. Ward," Kay returned flatly.

Sam Shults, shaking his head, said, "I'll leave it with you. I've got work to do." Neither Kay nor Sullivan responded. They never noticed when he left.

A deafening silence filled the corner office after Sam's departure. Like wary jungle cats, the two continued to silently size each other up, standing across from one another. Hands sliding deep into his pockets, Sullivan let his gaze leisurely glide over the small blond beauty looking at him.

The muscles of his stomach knotting painfully, Sullivan tried to keep his true emotions hidden. In truth, every natural impulse was to reach out and touch the glorious silvery hair, shining like a halo in the morning sun. His teeth clamped firmly together, his hands were clenching inside his pockets. How he longed to jerk the pins from her hair and let it spill down around her shoulders the way he liked it.

Those brilliant blue eyes were looking at him with that same wide-eyed innocence that had so devastated him before, and the perfect little turned-up nose was still adorable. The sweet mouth, even firmly compressed as it was now, had that soft, succulent look that made him want to pull her to him and kiss her senseless.

She was dressed more severely than when he'd last seen her. The tailored suit only hinted at the curves he knew were underneath. A muscle flexed in his jaw as his gaze slid over her high breasts, her narrow waist, her rounded hips. The desk between them hid those long, tanned legs from his view, but he had the distinct impression that she now wore hose, unlike the natural bare-legged girl of old. But now she was no girl. She was a sophisticated, twenty-four-year-old woman. And, God help him, she was more desirable than ever.

Slowly turning his back to Kay, he appeared to be peering out the window. In fact, his dark eyes were closed. To the majesty of the Rockies spread out before his shut eyes, he said, "Kay, have a chair."

Without answering, Kay took a seat, her eyes never leaving the raven-haired man with his back to her. Crossing her legs, Kay tugged at the tight skirt of her beige suit and pleaded with her heart to slow its furious beating.

Sullivan turned around.

The intensity had left the black eyes, but the coldness had not. "There's a few things we'll need to discuss." His tone was low, conversational, as he picked up a pack of cigarettes from atop his cluttered desk, then searched for a match. The gold lighter she'd given him on that last Christmas they spent together was nowhere in sight. Kay was not surprised.

Sullivan located a match at last, lit his cigarette and inhaled deeply. He sat down, lounging back in his swivel chair, his eyes on her. Kay cleared her throat needlessly and said, "It's great to be back in Denver, Sul—Sullivan."

"Is it?" He lifted a dark eyebrow and his mouth quirked into a hint of a derisive smile. "I'd think old Denver would be a bit tame for a lady who spent the last five years in L.A.''

"I'm a rather tame lady, or don't you remember?" Her level gaze met his.

Wide shoulders lifted slightly. Sullivan took another long drag from his cigarette, letting the smoke drift up around his face. "Ah, that's true, but then that was five years ago. I'm sure you've learned a lot, both professionally and personally." His eyes challenged her to deny it.

"Sullivan, I would certainly hope I've progressed professionally. If not, then I'm in the wrong line of work and I don't believe that is the case. It was you who first told me I had potential, talent, and that I should learn and polish and strive to get better each day, each year. That's exactly what I've done for the past five years." Kay took a needed breath and continued, hating the triumphant look on his smug face. She was squirming and he was quite obviously enjoying it immensely; it made her fingers itch to slap his hard swarthy cheek. "I am an air personality, Sullivan Ward, just as you are. There's nothing that makes me happier than being on the radio and I intend to spend the rest of my days doing what I love most."

Kay stopped speaking, her face flushed, blue eyes snapping. She crossed her arms over her chest and glared at him.

"All finished?" he asked amusedly, crushing out his cigarette. Her reply was a narrowing of her eyes. Sullivan shook his dark head. "Good, now that you've set me straight, maybe we can get on to the business at hand." Rising gracefully, he slid his hands into his pockets again and slowly circled his desk. Kay tensed as he neared her. He stepped directly in front of her chair and half sat, half leaned on his desk. "Where shall we begin?" he mused, looking down at her.

"Why don't you give me your little speech about you being the program director of this station and as such you do all the—"

"Damn you, Kay." He leaned menacingly close. "Sam Shults may have hired you back, but I'm your boss, do you understand me?" Those black eyes were flashing fire. Kay gripped the arms of her chair and wished she'd kept her glib tongue still. "I will indeed give you my speech and I'd advise you to listen. I'm not quite as easygoing as I once was and I can't be pushed around; not even by silver-haired beauties with big blue eyes and bigger egos. Be as ambitious as you please, Miss Clark, but as long as you're stuck here at Q102 awaiting your next big chance, you'll damned well do as I tell you. You may be the big star, Kay, but here at this particular radio station, I'll be the one—"

"Sullivan," Kay interrupted bravely, "will you just wait a—"

"No, Kay, I won't. We both know why you're here. Well, fair enough. Your career took a downturn, you lost your Los Angeles radio deal and you've come back down to the minor leagues for a while." Slowly, Sullivan leaned forward. He put a hand on either arm of Kay's chair, trapping her. His dark, handsome face was very close to hers. Cold black eyes impaled her and the smooth, velvet voice she loved so much said flatly, "How long do you plan to stay this time, Miss Clark? Three months? Six? Till you get a decent offer from some radio station in Chicago? Atlanta? Miami?"

Kay looked directly into his eyes. Anger rising rapidly, she lifted her small chin and smiled up at him. "Why, Sullivan—" she leaned closer to the hard-featured face above hers "—I've no intention of doing anything so foolish." She lowered her lids demurely; her smile widened and she looked back up at him. "Those cities would hardly be a step up, don't you agree?" She laughed and shook her silver head dismissively. "New York, Sullivan. The Big Apple. That would be the proper showcase for my talents, don't you think? That's where I belong."

Sullivan's dark eyes flickered dangerously for one brief instant. His hands left her chair and he stretched to his full, imposing height.

"Baby," he drawled, "that probably is where you belong. One thing is certain, you sure as hell don't belong here."

Kay rose before him, standing so close she had to tip her head back to look up at him. Longing to throw her arms around his neck, she wanted to confess that she never really wanted to be anywhere again but right here with him. She'd only said she belonged in New York in order to hurt him the way he'd hurt her. Kay watched the chiseled, hard face, the clenched jaw, the cruel eyes. His lean body was rigid, tensed. She had hoped some of the old warmth and feeling between them still remained, but she realized now the feelings were completely one-sided. Sullivan Ward didn't even regard her as a friend.

"All the same, Sullivan, I am here. I'm your partner once again on the morning show and I'll be in the control room at six o'clock tomorrow. Now, if you'd like to run through a practice play set, or discuss our first show, I'll sit back down and we'll go about this like two intelligent professionals. If not, I'll be going."

Sullivan nodded. "Let's play it by ear in the morning. Might make the show fresher."

"Good enough," Kay agreed, turned and walked to the door. Pausing, she turned to look back at him. "Sullivan?"

"Yes?"

"I see you still have your chinning bar." She smiled, looking up at the steel cylinder stretching across from north wall to south.

"Yeah," he said, a hint of a smile on his mouth. "Not many changes around here, I guess." He inclined his head in a sweeping gesture. "My office is pretty much like it was when you left."

Kay noted the framed awards and gold records dotting the wall. The records were recognition for being the first disc jockey in the country to break a hit record on the air. The awards were for various honors, and for achievements Sullivan had made in the field of broadcasting. A long leather couch, custom-built for the tall man who sometimes used it for a bed, still sat in place beneath a wide mirror reaching almost to the ceiling. A closed interior door led into Sullivan's private bath. He'd often joked that his salary was not the most important consideration in his employment contract. A chinning bar and a shower were. Without those two items, Sullivan Ward refused to work.

The only thing missing from the old days were the many color photographs of her. All had been removed from the walls, from the credenza, from his desk. Not a trace of her remained.

"Do you still chin yourself when something's bothering you?" Kay smiled, recalling the way Sullivan spent a lot of time lifting himself up to the chinning bar when he had a particular problem.

Sullivan's face colored beneath the darkness of his complexion and he ignored her question. His voice soft and modulated, he said, "See you in the morning, Kay."

"Yes," she said, "in the morning."

When Kay left Sullivan's office and stepped into the corridor, a smiling, attractive woman materialized from an office next door. She smiled warmly at Kay.

"Miss Clark, I'm Janelle Davis, Sullivan's secretary. If you'll just come with me, I'll show you to your office."

"Thank you, Janelle." Kay followed the tall, slim woman with short brown hair and warm gray eyes. Janelle Davis looked to be about Sullivan's age. She was attractive, well-groomed and pleasant. She directed Kay to a small office all the way down the hall from Sullivan's. A keen female intuition told Kay that this tall woman was very fond of Sullivan Ward. That suspicion was confirmed when Janelle, helping Kay settle into the new office, spoke of him. A warm light came into her expressive gray eyes when she mentioned his name. Kay could tell the woman was trying very hard to hide the jealousy she was experiencing because of Kay's arrival back on the scene.

"I've tried to stock your desk with anything you may need, Miss Clark," Janelle was saying.

"Please, Janelle, call me Kay. And thanks for your help. It seems you've thought of everything." Kay smiled and looked at the neatly stacked notepads, sharpened pencils, ballpoint pens. There was even a crystal bud vase on the corner of her teak desk.

Hands clasped together, Janelle smiled back at Kay. "I've labeled the buttons on your phone. If you need to speak to Sullivan, press my number and I'll put you through to him," Janelle said possessively.

"I'll do that, Janelle," Kay assured her. "And let's have lunch together soon."

"Sure," Janelle agreed and backed out, closing the door behind her. Janelle had hardly made her exit before Kay's line was buzzing.

Kay's well-shaped brows lifted in puzzlement and she raised the phone to her ear. "Hi," came the bubbly female voice, "this is Sherry. . . you know, the receptionist."

"Hi, Sherry, what's up?"

"I've just got a minute, the phones are real busy, you know. I'm calling about lunch. Want to go over to Leo's with me at noon?"

Kay bit her lip and hesitated. If it were like the old days, all the jocks would be at Leo's, including Sullivan. "Sherry, I don't know."

"Oh, Kay. I'm dying to hear all about Los Angeles, I've never been there and please say you'll go. I'll even buy."

Kay laughed. "You'll do no such thing, Sherry, but I'll be delighted to go to lunch with you. Sure you wouldn't like to go someplace other than Leo's?"

Disappointment in her voice, Sherry said pleadingly, "But, Kay, I want everyone to see you with me. Gosh, that'll be half the fun."

"Leo's it is." Kay was won over by the guileless charm of the impressionable young woman. "And it's my treat."

Leo's place was just across Broadway, but by the time the two women reached the heavy mahogany door with its oval stained-glass inset, Sherry had, unasked, filled Kay in on almost everything presently going on at Q102.

"And I personally believe that Sullivan's secretary—did you meet her yet—is absolutely crazy for him and he thinks a lot of her, of course, she's so kind and efficient. They have dinner together at least once a week, but actually I don't think Sullivan considers her as anything other than a close friend.'' Sherry paused for a quick breath and hurried on, "He's strange. I mean, he's such a handsome hunk and all the women just go all weak-kneed over him, me included, and sure, I've seen him out with some really beautiful ladies, but none of them last very long. It's downright puzzling.'' Sherry's auburn brows knitted for one second, then she smiled warmly. "He's never given me a second thought, treats me like a kid sister, you know, he's always teasing me and he can be loads of fun when he's not... Then, lately, I don't know, he's been short-tempered. I don't understand it. Oh, and too, you know that chinning bar in his office? Well, for the last week or so he's always hanging on the darned thing. I have to buzz and buzz to get him to the phone and I know it's because he's chinning.'' They were at the door of the restaurant, much to Kay's relief. "By the way—'' Sherry grinned "—Jeff Kerns, he's Sullivan's best friend, he says that—''

"Jeff's still here?'' Kay was overjoyed with the news. Lovable, witty Jeff Kerns had been at Q102 as long as Sullivan Ward, which was at least a dozen years. The two men had grown up together and had moved from their home state of Montana to Denver to begin their broadcasting careers. "I can't wait to see him.''

"Jeff will probably be inside.'' Sherry tugged open the heavy door and followed Kay into the dim room. Kay's eyes scanned the familiar, intimate restaurant where she'd spent so many pleasant hours seated next to Sullivan. She'd listen almost reverently while he, his long arm draped possessively around her shoulders, had talked of music, promotions and talent with the assembled crew of disc jockeys and salespeople and secretaries from the radio station.

The restaurant wasn't crowded today. The heavy luncheon traffic had thinned and many of the tables in the cozy downtown restaurant and bar were empty. High-backed wooden booths still held a few late diners, and the long polished bar to the left of the black-and-white tiled entrance was occupied with a few drinkers, mostly young executives who worked in the downtown Denver skyscrapers.

"C.A.!" Kay heard Jeff's familiar voice shouting from a table in the very back of the room. She smiled. Jeff never called her Kay. On that first long-ago day when Sullivan had introduced her to his best buddy, Jeff Kerns had looked her over with unabashed approval, letting his twinkling blue eyes come to rest on her hair. And he'd stated softly, as though he were thinking aloud, "You've the hair of a Christmas angel." Then he'd grinned, shook her hand warmly and said, "That's exactly what you look like, honey, a beautiful Christmas angel. I'll call you C.A. for short."

Jeff was making his way toward her, grinning from ear to ear. Snatching from his head a white sailor cap, he crushed it in one hand and threw his arms wide open. "C.A., you little doll, you're prettier than ever." He gave her cheek an affectionate kiss.

"Jeff, it's great to see you again." Kay was beaming happily at the man who held her in a bear hug. Then, over his shoulder, she noticed a glowering Sullivan Ward looking directly at her. Sullivan's eyes lowered the minute she saw him, but Kay knew he didn't want her here and she wished she'd persuaded Sherry to go someplace else for lunch. It was too late now.

The outgoing Jeff had positioned himself between the two women and was propelling them to the table of station employees, saying to Sherry, "Now this changes nothing between us, Sherry, honey, but you'll have to understand I've been in love with C.A. for years. You'll just have to learn to share." His impish eyes sparkled with his teasing.

"You're full of it," Sherry responded goodnaturedly and smiled at the table full of men, all rising to acknowledge the presence of ladies. Kay's eyes automatically went to Sullivan. He rose more slowly than the others, as though he resented the intrusion.

Jeff, paying no attention to the less than pleasant expression on Sullivan's face, said pointedly, "You can get lost, Ward. C.A. is going to sit by me." He pulled out a chair and handed her down into it. "Sherry, why don't you scoot in over there between Sullivan and Dallas?"

When everyone was again seated, Jeff looked across the table at Sullivan and said, "This'll be a good time for C.A. to meet the crew."

His dark eyes hidden beneath lowered lashes, Sullivan said without looking up, "Do the honors, will you, Jeffrey?" His gaze slowly lifted to Kay. "You introduce Kay."

"Glad to, oh Great One," Jeff quipped irreverently, pressing his palms together as one in prayer, bowing humbly over his steepled hands. Kay laughed at Jeff's antics, as did everyone else at the table. She glanced nervously at Sullivan. His full mouth lifted into a grin; Kay relaxed a little.

"First of all, gang," Jeff announced loudly, "C.A. does not stand for what you think. It's Christmas angel; so keep that fact in mind, and no wisecracks, okay?" All laughed and Jeff winked at Kay. "C.A., my only love, that healthy-looking blond fellow at the other end of the table is Dallas Knight; Dallas handles the 10:00 p.m. to 2:00 a.m. slot."

Nodding to her, the blond man smiled engagingly at Kay. "Welcome aboard, Kay. Need anything, you let me know."

"Thank you, Dallas." Kay liked his friendly face and manner.

"Across from old Dallas," Jeff continued, "is Dale of Darkness, real name Dale Kitrell. He's on the air from 2:00 a.m. until 6:00, when you and Sullivan come in to relieve him." Jeff leaned closer to Kay and conspiratorially said in a stage whisper, "Dale's weird, so stay clear of him. He's spent too much time alone every night; I'm afraid it's taken a toll. He talks to trees."

Smiling at Jeff's description, Dale Kitrell winked at Kay. "Jeff is understandably jealous of me, Kay. It's not simply a case of my superior talent, it's that I have all this thick, healthy hair, while as you can see, Jeff's is rapidly thinning." Dale ran a slender hand through his unruly red hair and grinned so broadly that all the freckles around his big green eyes ran together.

Kay laughed. "Glad to meet you, Dale. I'll be listening to your show when I get up in the morning. And your hair is gorgeous, no wonder Jeff's jealous.'' She turned back to Jeff, still smiling.

Frowning, Jeff pretended dismay. "Jealous? Who's jealous? Seems I recall something about bald-headed men being more virile...hell, I can't wait till I lose it all. My sweet little wife says I get sexier every year." He playfully growled at Kay before retrieving his wadded sailor cap from his pocket, setting it on his head and pulling it down over his impish blue eyes.

"Yeah," Dale reminded Jeff, "but it's my little wife that's pregnant again."

Ignoring Dale's statement, Jeff said, "That youth over there that looks like he just got weaned last week is the midday man, Ace Black...get it? His real name is Bill Smith or something equally dull." Ace, nineteen years old, tall, lanky, extremely shy, nodded to Kay.

The introductions continued. Kay met, in addition to the disc jockeys, two of the newsmen, the chief engineer and a couple of the top salespeople. All were polite, friendly and new to Kay. None had been at Q102 when she'd worked there before. They were obviously delighted to be a part of the congenial staff of Q102. Kay wanted to be as delighted as they, but while spirited conversation erupted all around her, Kay hazarded a glance at Sullivan Ward.

He was silent. His long fingers were wrapped tightly around a glass of beer. He was looking straight at her. His eyes darkened when she held his gaze. They sat quietly looking at each other and Kay, holding her breath, was relieved when Sherry, seated beside Sullivan, tugged on his sleeve, distracting him.

"Sullivan," Sherry chattered happily, "I just think it's so wonderful that you and Kay are going to be partners again, don't you? Just think of all the fun you two will have making personal appearances. Gosh, you look so great together. She's so beautiful and nice, not the least bit stuck-up. What's that you're eating?" Her hazel eyes went to the untouched plate in front of him.

"Prime rib," Sullivan said, glancing at the shiny gold watch on his wrist. "I'm out of time," he said abruptly, pushing back his chair.

"But, Sullivan," Sherry pouted, "you can't leave. You haven't touched your food."

He rose. His eyes were once again on Kay. "I'm not hungry," he said truthfully, and Kay wished she could be as honest. That was Sullivan. He always said what was on his mind.

Without another word, Sullivan nodded to the people around the long table, turned and strolled toward the door. Kay watched him go. His long strides were sure, graceful, but determined. There was no doubt in her mind that he left because she'd joined the group. She sighed when his tall frame went out the door.

Kay ordered a salad and pushed it around on her plate while she laughed and talked with Jeff, Sherry and the rest of the staff. But she was relieved when the time finally came for Sherry to get back to her reception desk. Declining Jeff's invitation to hang around while he had one more beer, Kay returned to the radio station with Sherry and went directly to her small office, closing the door behind her.

She'd no sooner placed her handbag in the bottom drawer of her desk than her phone rang. "Yes?" she said shakily.

"Kay, it's Sam," came the coarse, booming voice. "Hon, I just wanted to let you know that Benny Brown, our best salesman, just came in with the keys to the car he got for you over at the Porsche dealership." Kay smiled. The new car was part of the deal she'd made in her new contract with Q102. Sam Shults hadn't flinched when she'd asked for it. It was common practice for successful radio stations to trade advertising time on the air for goods and services. Sam had known that providing her with a car would be as simple as calling on a dealer and offering time on Q102. "Kay, honey," Sam continued, "a Porsche is all right, isn't it?"

"Sammy, I think I'll be able to make do." She laughed. "I'm thrilled to death, who wouldn't be?"

"Good, Kay, I was just afraid . . . well, Sullivan has a big gray Mercedes and I didn't want you to think . . ."

"Sam, I think a Mercedes is just right for Sullivan. I'm more than pleased with a Porsche, believe me."

"You're a sweetheart, but then you always were." Sam sounded relieved. "Anyway, it's downstairs in the parking lot. I've got the keys when you're ready to leave."

"As a matter of fact," Kay said thoughtfully, "I need to start hunting for an apartment, so if it's all right with you, I think I'll leave for the day and spend the rest of the afternoon looking at a few places."

"Do that, Kay. Want me to call Betty and have her come to town and help you?"

"You're sweet, but no. I don't think I'll have too much trouble finding something I like...Sammy, does Sullivan still live over at the Park Lane Towers by Washington Park?"

"Sure does. Why don't you ask him if they have anything available?"

"Hmm," she said, "I will. See you in five minutes for those car keys." Kay hung up the phone. "So he still lives atop the Park Lane Towers," she said aloud. She retrieved her handbag and left her office, thinking she'd hunt for a place to live as far from the Park Lane Towers as possible.

Kay stepped into the hall just as Sullivan's secretary, Janelle Davis, opened the door of Sullivan's office. Janelle stood in the portal, speaking to him, holding the heavy door half open. Kay walked nearer and overheard what the tall, attractive woman was saying.

"Must you continue doing that, Sullivan? We really need to handle some correspondence." Janelle Davis's voice was softly scolding.

Kay couldn't help herself. As she drew closer to Sullivan's door, her betraying gaze went past Janelle and into the room. She got only a fleeting glimpse before she tore her eyes away, turned and rushed through the reception area toward Sam Shults's office.

But even after she'd picked up the keys to her brand-new red Porsche, and left, she was still seeing Sullivan, shirtless, a sheen of perspiration covering his bare torso, chinning himself.

Outside, Kay hurried down the sidewalk to the pay parking beside the Petroleum Club building where the shiny new Porsche awaited. She reached the low-slung car, unlocked the door and paused. Slowly she threw back her head. Eyes squinting in the glaring September sun, Kay lifted a hand to shade them. She looked straight up for an instant, searching out the tall windows at the very top of the building.

Carefully counting across, she located Sullivan's. She saw nothing, no one, and yet she had the eerie feeling that he'd swung gracefully down from that steel chinning rod and was at his window watching her. That he'd caught her foolishly looking up.

Kay jerked the car door open and lunged into the low leather seat of the new automobile. Fingers shaking, she jammed the keys into the ignition, started the powerful engine and roared out of the parking lot as though the devil himself were after her.

Three

—

At four-thirty the next morning, the clock radio beside Kay's bed came on. Kay blinked, looked around and snuggled deeper into the blue sheets. The room was pitch-black; it was much too early for anyone to get up. Eyes closing again, Kay heard Dale Kitrell, the all-night man at Q102, saying in a deep, pleasant voice, "So if there's anyone out there, I'm playing this one for you. It's 'Hold Me' by Fleetwood Mac. Wish somebody would hold me," Dale growled and turned up the music.

Kay, remembering the slim, red-haired man, opened her eyes, smiled sleepily and rose. Lazily divesting herself of her pajamas, she pulled a plastic shower cap over her hair and stepped into the shower. Sighing, she stood under the pelting spray, letting its warmth bring her fully awake.

With awareness came apprehension. It was to be her first morning back on the air with Sullivan. Kay turned around in the steamy shower, letting the water pepper her back while she idly slid a soapy washcloth over her body.

How would they behave? Would the old magic that they'd once shared still be there? Would they still be able to look into each other's eyes and know exactly what the other one was going to say? Kay trembled. What they'd had then was so free and easy, yet so powerful and effective. They'd been the golden couple, effortlessly charming their listening audience from that dim control room that was their stage.

Kay smiled wistfully as she lathered her slender arms. How many times had she and Sul sat behind the control board teasing, touching, even kissing. It had been a game to try to make the other lose composure. Kay's smile broadened. What fun they'd had then, what pure, undiluted joy with each other and the work they loved doing.

Kay turned around, lifted her face to the watery needles, finished her shower and stepped out of the marble stall. Drying her body on a thirsty blue towel, she padded back into the bedroom. She drew a pair of pantyhose from the top drawer of the bureau, leaned over to inhale the still-fresh roses and walked back to the unmade bed.

She sat down on its edge and she wondered. Was Sullivan now stepping from his shower in his penthouse apartment across town? Was that tall, spare body glistening wet and smelling of soap? Was the ebony hair damp and shiny? Was that crisp mat of hair on his broad, dark chest beaded with water?

Kay shivered and stepped into her pantyhose, frantically jerking them up over her hips and quivering stomach. Hose in place, she almost ran to the dresser to seek a bra, eager to cover naked, swelling breasts whose nipples were becoming taut.

Kay arrived at the studios of Q102 half an hour early. Dressed sensibly in an attractive cowl-necked cotton dress of gold and blue stripes, a wide blue leather belt and matching shoes, she used her key to let herself into the dim reception area. It was eerily quiet, as were the empty sales offices opening into it.

Kay's heels made no sound as she crossed the lobby and headed down the long corridor toward her office. Suddenly the hair stood up on the back of her neck. She could sense someone behind her. She whirled around so abruptly she bumped into the hard chest of Sullivan Ward.

Kay let out a little gasp of surprise. Sullivan's hands were on her upper arms, steadying her. Eyes on the level of his throat, Kay's senses were assailed with the dizzyingly irresistible scent of his clean, warm skin. Instinctively, she inhaled deeply, loving the familiar yet strange male essence that was Sul. Her Sul.

Abruptly, his long fingers encircling her arms, Sullivan set her away from him. Kay looked up at his face. In his eyes was an enigmatic expression. It fled immediately and a look of impatience replaced it.

"I—I didn't hurt you, did I?" she asked, as his hands left her.

A mocking grin lifted the corners of his lips. "What do you think?" he said flatly. He turned and walked away from her. Kay stood rooted to the spot, dumbly watching him head for his office. The way the linen trousers he wore clung to his slim hips commanded her attention briefly, then her eyes slid upward to those wide, chiseled shoulders and the white cotton shirt stretching across them. His shoulder blades were sliding upward a little as though he were shrugging about something.

Kay bit her bottom lip. This was not going to work. Not at all. An unhappy Sullivan was going to make this first show a disaster. She just knew it. They could no longer work together. She should never have returned.

At two minutes before six, Kay left her small office. At the opposite end of the hall, Sullivan did the same. They met at the door to the control room. Wordlessly, Sullivan put a palm to the door and pushed it inward, inclining his dark head.

Just as silently, Kay nodded and stepped past him into the room where bleary-eyed Dale Kitrell was signing off his show. Nodding to the pair, the tired disc jockey said into the microphone, "So that's it for the night people. Be listening again when yours truly, Dale of Darkness, comes back your way in the dead of night." The weary man turned up the volume, letting the last record lead into the 6 o'clock news.

"Hi, folks." He rose, yawned and stretched long arms over his head.

"Good morning, Dale." Kay smiled at him while Sullivan reached out and shook his hand.

As soon as Dale was gone, Sullivan walked behind the control board, drew a second chair up beside the one Dale Kitrell had just vacated and looked at Kay. "Think you can fill out the federal communications log if I handle everything else?"

Kay slowly circled the control panel. Purposely walking past the first chair, she took the seat directly in front of the console. Swiveling around, she looked up at him and said calmly, "Not only can I handle the FCC log, Sullivan, I can run the board as well. I will cue and spin the records, position and play the tapes and run the proper commercials." She smiled sweetly and added, "You just have a seat beside me and charm your listeners. I'm fully trained to handle all of this." Her small hands made a sweeping gesture around the glass-enclosed room with its racks of records, carousel of tapes and cartridges and the latest in electronic equipment.

"Fine," Sullivan said evenly, reaching for a clean FCC log and dropping it before her. Sliding down into the seat beside her, he folded his arms across his chest and leaned lazily back in his chair.

Ignoring him, Kay reached out to spin the cassette carousel, rapidly familiarizing herself with the color-coded dots designating the A, B and C songs. Turning back to Sullivan, she said crisply, "Where's the playlist, Sullivan?"

"Why, Kay—" his eyes lifted to hers "—this is Q102. We don't play the hits here. We make 'em, remember?"

"Yes, I know, but what shall I—"

"It's thirty seconds till time, better pick something." Sullivan slowly leaned forward and pulled the mike into position. Heart hammering in her chest, Kay snatched a blue-dotted cassette from its place and shoved it into the recorder just as Sullivan flipped open the key and said in that smooth, sexy voice, "Morning, sleepyheads. It's your old buddy, Sullivan Ward. The day we've all been waiting for has finally arrived. Sure, I know every day we spend here together in this beautiful state of Colorado is special, but there's magic in the Mile High City today."

Sullivan's brooding black eyes went to Kay as he continued. "I'm sure a lot of you remember the beautiful and talented Kay Clark. Kay was my morning-show partner back in the good old days here at Q102. Well, she's back and I couldn't be happier. It's just like old times around here. For those who have moved to Denver in the past five years, I'll see if I can't describe Kay for you. She's about five feet three inches tall and...call it a hundred and two pounds, all in the right places." His eyes were slowly sliding over Kay as he spoke.

"She has the hair of a Christmas angel, all long and silvery. Her eyes are cobalt blue and so enormous you could lose yourself in them. Her nose is turned up just a bit and her lips are...what can I tell you...they're soft and sweet and—oh, I can't go on. She's Kay Clark, she's breathtaking, she's talented and she's mine. Did I say mine? She's yours, friends, and she's delighted to be back here in this glorious jewel of the Rockies, our home and hers, Denver, Colorado. Say hello, Kay."

Face flushing hotly from his unwavering scrutiny and the overly complimentary introduction, Kay swallowed nervously, leaned closer to the mike and, looking directly into the watchful eyes of Sullivan, said confidently, "Thank you, Sullivan. Hello, Colorado. You'll never know how overjoyed I am to once again be in my beloved Denver and back on the morning show at Q102 with the talented man who taught me all I know."

Kay saw the brief flicker in Sullivan's hooded eyes and quickly amended, "About broadcasting, that is." Hand trembling ever so slightly, Kay clutched the mike and concluded, "I'll be seeing all of you old friends real soon, since Sullivan and I plan to be making lots of personal appearances. Keep listening and give us a call now and then to let us know you're there. Now how about a little music?'' Kay pushed a button and music filled the control room.

While the sound of Linda Ronstadt's voice permeated the air, Kay checked the time, wrote it on the FCC log and turned to hunt for the tape for the first scheduled commercial. Sullivan, once again leaning back in his chair, grudgingly admired her. The correct commercial located, she pulled a record from its jacket and expertly cued it on the turntable. That done, she turned and stole a glance at her partner.

Sullivan looked into those dazzling blue eyes, slowly leaned forward and softly said, ''Let me help.'' For one heart-stopping moment his big hand covered her trembling one and Kay felt his strength, his warmth.

''Th—thank you,'' she stammered when that strong, male hand gently squeezed hers.

''You're welcome, Kay.'' His voice was low, sincere. ''We'll do it together, hon, uh, Kay.'' His hand left hers and a long arm shot out behind her to pull several color-coded tapes from the carousel. ''These are some of the best, I think. Be good for the first segment of the show.'' He smiled at her and Kay felt her heart take wing.

Half an hour later, the phone in the control booth began ringing off the wall. Raves poured in. Listeners loved the easy banter and great rapport between the man and woman talking to each other in a relaxed and often humorous manner. Their timing was perfect, as though they'd never been apart. They could practically read one another's minds. One would begin a sentence; the other would finish. While they joked, two wide sky-blue eyes were often locked with a pair of blazing black ones.

The fire between them still burned.

At least in the control room of the radio station. Both felt the powerful electricity flowing from one to the other and both experienced a physical charge from it. Pushing each other higher and higher, they delighted in the playful challenge of their verbal duel. Both felt gloriously awake and vitally stimulated by the all-or-nothing contest as each strove to be on par, if not to surpass, the wit and repartee of the other.

Adding to the exciting exercise of keen intellects, an undeniable physical attraction still existed between them. It not only filled the tiny space they occupied, making both Sullivan and Kay feel warm, animated, titillated; it magically transmitted itself over the airwaves and into homes and cars. Listeners felt they were experiencing a very special happening and they delighted in it.

Sullivan and Kay took turns answering the busy phones, cuing the records, logging the commercials and talking into their mikes. The four-hour show flew past and Kay was shocked when Sullivan said, "Lead 'em into the last song, Kay, it's two minutes till ten."

Smiling at him, Kay complied and when the last record came up in volume, she turned to him; happy, relieved, longing for his approval.

"You're good, Kay. Very good, better than ever," he said, shaking his dark head.

Kay instinctively reached out and put a hand on his dark forearm. "I should be," she said softly, leaning toward him, "you taught me all I know."

Feeling the ripple of hard, taut muscles beneath his shirt sleeve, Kay drew a sharp breath when Sullivan, ignoring her accolade, asked casually, "Have you got anything planned for this coming Saturday morning?"

They didn't work on Saturdays. Kay's fingers tightened a little on Sullivan's arm as excitement filled her small body.

"Why, no, I don't, Sullivan," she said in a whisper. "I've nothing at all planned, nothing to do."

"Good," he responded dryly, brushing her hand from his arm. "There's to be a charity touch-football game Saturday morning at ten between Q102 and channel ten television. Be a good idea if you'd agree to play."

Disappointed, Kay stared up at him and stammered, "I... why, sure, I'll be glad to do it."

Sullivan walked away. "Come by my office and get a T-shirt with the station call letters. You own a pair of white shorts, I'm sure."

"Yes, but why can't I wear jeans?"

Sullivan paused at the door. "This is show biz, babe. People listen to you and turn out to see you in person. They want to look at you in a tight T-shirt and a pair of shorts that show off your long, tanned legs."

"Well—" Kay followed him, saying indignantly "—maybe I don't want to show off my legs and my...my..."

"Come off it, Kay," Sullivan said coldly. "You rode in a Los Angeles parade in a damned brief bikini that almost showed your...your..." He slammed out of the door and was gone.

Kay, face pink, hands balled into fists at her sides, gritted her teeth, stormed out into the hall and to the privacy of her small office. It was not until she'd fumed for several minutes, pacing back and forth before the tall windows, that she stopped abruptly and wondered aloud, "How did Sullivan know about a parade I was in four years ago? And why has he remembered it all this time?"

Kay stood on the sunny balcony of her new high-rise apartment overlooking Cheeseman Park and dried her long, silvery hair while sipping a glass of freshly squeezed orange juice.

It was Saturday morning. The week had passed quickly; the hours spent on the air with Sullivan had been exciting, fun, like old times. Off the air, it was a different story. Sullivan had little to do with her and his black mood had gone unnoticed by no one. Bubbly Sherry had commented bluntly that she'd never seen Sullivan so bad-tempered. Ever-patient Janelle Davis had once been seen leaving his office near to tears, and even Sam Shults had dropped in on Kay to quiz her about Sullivan's disagreeable behavior.

Only Jeff Kerns seemed unmoved by Sullivan's frequent outbursts and long silences. Jeff was in and out of Sullivan's office just as he had always been, and more often than not shouting could be heard through the closed door. Jeff would exit, smiling as though nothing undue had taken place.

Kay was all too aware that Sullivan's bad humor was because she was back, but the depth of his displeasure was puzzling. She could understand his being resentful. She'd been young and very ambitious. When she'd been offered a slot at one of L.A.'s top radio stations, she'd been thrilled and flattered. She'd accepted the offer, leaving their successful team show, despite the fact that she was in love with Sullivan Ward.

Over and over again she'd asked Sullivan if she was doing the right thing by taking the offered west-coast job. Each time she'd hoped he'd beg her to stay in Denver. She'd prayed he'd say that he loved her and couldn't bear to let her go. But he never had. His answer was always that it was a great opportunity and that she should make up her own mind.

Even on that last night, when Sullivan had made love to her for the first and last time, he still did not tell her to stay. Not even when she'd lain trustingly in his arms.

Kay shook her head, rose and went inside to dress for the charity football game. Unaware of just how attractive she looked, Kay, in a snug red T-shirt with "Q102" splashed across it, tight white shorts exposing her long, tanned legs and silver hair pushed up under a crimson baseball cap, swept through the glass double doors of Q102 forty-five minutes before game time.

Other Q102 employees, dressed identically to Kay, were milling around in the reception area, laughing, drinking coffee and eating doughnuts. Sherry Jones spotted Kay and immediately flew over to meet her. "Kay, you look gorgeous." Sherry's sparkling green eyes swept over Kay's trim figure. "I wish I were slender like you. I didn't eat a bit of supper for the last two nights hoping I'd lose five pounds by this morning so I'd look good in these shorts, but it didn't happen." Sherry pouted prettily and twisted a long strand of her auburn hair around a finger.

"You look great, Sherry," Kay assured her, smiling and let her eyes slide casually around the room, looking for Sullivan. She saw him and her breath caught in her throat. He was at the far side of the room speaking to Jeff and a couple of the jocks. He was dressed like her, except the colors were reversed. His T-shirt was snowy white, his shorts fire-engine red, his cap white.

If ever a man looked disturbingly sexy, Sullivan Ward did this morning. Halfheartedly listening to Sherry, Kay guiltily stole glances at the tall, ruggedly handsome man while he remained unaware of her perusal. Something Jeff said made Sullivan break into a dazzling laugh, his black eyes flashing with amusement.

A hand went up to shove the white baseball cap back on his head, releasing curly raven locks that fell casually over his high forehead. The movement of his arm sent muscles rippling beneath the tightly stretched white T-shirt and no sooner had his hand dropped from the bill of his cap than it went unselfconsciously underneath his shirt to scratch idly at a hard, flat abdomen.

Kay had given up pretending to listen to Sherry. While the young woman's cheerful voice went on and on, Kay, her breathing at a premium, was drawn by Sullivan's unintentionally sensual performance. Her eyes were glued to the bare stomach he was thoughtlessly exposing. She was caught.

As though he could feel her gaze, his eyes went over Jeff's head and came to rest on her. The laughter left his full lips; the light died in his black eyes. The long, lean fingers stilled on his stomach and fell away. A muscle tightened in his jaw as he quietly regarded her. Trapped, Kay smiled weakly at him. He returned the gesture, but it was restrained, indifferent.

"Okay, people." Sam Shults came out of his office and everyone broke into laughter and applause. Sam was in uniform, too, although not the kind worn by the rest of the team. Instead, the rotund little man wore a chauffeur's uniform. He stood, face beet-red, being a good sport, while his staff jeered, whistled and clapped. Sam, his double-breasted black suit, tall shiny boots and billed cap making him appear more foolish than if he'd been wearing shorts and a T-shirt, was nodding his head, laughingly acknowledging the absurdity of his appearance.

"I don't understand," Kay whispered in Sherry's ear.

"Isn't it great?" Sherry leaned close. "Mr. Shults is going to drive the limousine we're riding in to the stadium."

"You're pulling my leg."

"No, really. It's all part of the promotion. The team is to ride over in a couple of limos. Channel ten's team is doing the same thing. Mr. Shults and Sullivan thought it would be a great idea if the general manager played the part of chauffeur."

Kay smiled and her blue eyes went to Sam Shults. That was Sammy. Anything for Q102 radio.

Sam raised his arms in the air for quiet. "Okay, okay." He bobbed his head. "You've had your laugh. Now it's time to go. The limos are waiting downstairs." His eyes swept the sea of smiling faces. "I don't care who rides where, but I will tell you this, it'll make me mad as hell if no one climbs into the car I'll be driving. Let's go."

Two long black stretch Mercedes limousines were waiting at the curb outside the Petroleum Club building. Amidst laughter and shouts, the team was piling into the plush seats. Kay was never quite certain how it happened, but she found herself in the very back seat next to a withdrawn Sullivan Ward.

He was beside the door, a long arm draped along the back of the seat. More people climbed into the car and Kay was pushed closer to Sullivan. She could feel his muscles tighten tensely when she stole a glance up at his face from beneath silky lowered lashes. He was staring out the window, a distant look on his face.

"Hey." It was Jeff's voice. "Come on in here, Dallas. Sherry can sit closer to me." He turned and looked at Kay. "C.A., crawl up there on Sullivan's knees, will you, we've got to get some more warm bodies in this seat."

"But I—" Kay began lamely just as Jeff jerked her up and unceremoniously deposited her upon the unoffered lap of a scowling Sullivan. Sullivan's dark head turned from the window just as Kay was thrust upon him. Their faces almost bumped; their eyes caught, and Kay shuddered at his fierce expression.

"I'm sorry, Sullivan, I didn't mean—"

He turned to look back out of the window, mumbling unconvincingly, "Doesn't matter."

All the heavy doors slammed shut. "Shall we be off?" Sam Shults said over his uniformed shoulder. Putting the car in gear he jerkily pulled away from the curb. The high-spirited passengers began to sing loudly as Sam headed for the valley highway.

Two passengers did not sing along.

Once on the freeway, Sam accelerated the powerful car. He increased the speed so rapidly that Kay, who'd been perching precariously on Sullivan's hard knees determined not to touch him any more than was necessary, was thrown helplessly back against him.

Immediately she was apologizing and struggling to sit up. Flattening a hand to his broad chest to push herself away, she said, "Sullivan, I didn't mean to." She was up again, perched on his knees.

Sullivan sighed, smiled and gallantly pulled her back down to him. "It's all right. Get comfortable, we've a way to go. Put your arm around me and hold on before you get hurt."

Gratefully, Kay did. She cautiously draped an arm around his shoulders, lightly clutching his neck. To her surprise, Sullivan's long arms came around her and he gently settled her close to his warm chest.

It was paradise. It was hell.

Soon they reached the stadium. Together, Sullivan and Kay ran onto the field to the approving applause of thousands of cheering fans. Waving and throwing kisses to a crowd much larger than either had dreamed of, the golden couple, wearing dazzling smiles, slowed to move along the stands, cheerfully signing autographs and shaking hands.

The blowing of the referee's whistle found the center for the Q102 team bent down over the ball, hands firmly on the pigskin, knees bent, bottom pointed skyward, ready to snap the ball to the waiting quarterback. The quarterback, lean brown hands reaching between the legs of the nervous center, called the play in a deep and commanding voice.

Kay snapped the ball to Sullivan and the game between the Q102 Spinners and the Channel Ten Glossies was underway. Sullivan rapidly backpedaled, the ball held in his strong right hand. Kay, not quite certain what she was to do now that she'd handed him the football, ran toward the opponents, looking back over her shoulder at Sullivan.

Sullivan pumped once, then threw a spiraling pass to Jeff Kerns. Perfectly thrown, the ball landed right on target and Jeff, after catching it, managed to run five yards before he was tagged by a laughing anchorwoman from the channel ten news team.

Kay clapped happily, lined up for the next play and bent over the ball, clasping it on the ground. She let her eyes slide up to the pair of well-tended brown hands in position between her legs. Those hands belonged to Sullivan and he was hunched so closely over her she could feel his body heat, his breath. Kay shivered, bit her lip and looked back down at the ball, determined to keep her thoughts solely on the game.

Sullivan, his lean body bent close to Kay's, tried just as desperately to keep his mind on the game. It was difficult with that cute rear, clad only in white shorts, pointed in the air. It was agony to put his hands near those creamy thighs, waiting to receive a snapped ball, when what he really wanted to do was stroke and caress the soft and temptingly touchable flesh. It was extremely hard to lean close to her slender back, his eyes helplessly drawn to the fragile nape of her neck where wisps of silver hair, coming loose from under her cap, curled seductively against damp flesh. It was all he could do to keep from lowering his lips to press heated kisses there, mindless of the thousands of people looking on.

The game continued and Sullivan's performance rapidly deteriorated from brilliant to just plain lousy. His passes missed the mark by a mile. He fumbled the snap more than once. He was tagged far behind the line of scrimmage nu-

merous times. Before the first quarter had ended, channel
ten was leading Q102 by a score of seventeen to nothing.

Only Sullivan, and perhaps Kay, knew where the problem lay. When Sullivan unceremoniously informed Kay he
was changing her playing position, that she would switch
with Rita from accounting, Kay merely nodded, though
Rita, disappointed, protested. Unmoved, Sullivan told Rita
it was for the good of the team. The trade took place.

Sullivan relaxed and became the formidable competitor
he'd been in past years. Kay was delighted with her new position and when, later in the game, Sullivan threw a perfectly aimed pass into her upraised waiting hands, Kay
squealed with delight and took off running for the goal line.
She'd gone only a few yards before a muscular blond salesman on the channel ten team caught up with her.

He grabbed for her T-shirt, pulling it hard, and Kay, excitement and momentum carrying her, forgot it was only
touch football. She tried to wrench away from the grinning, good-looking Dave Kelso. She heard the tear of her
shirt just as she hit the grassy ground. The big blond man
came crashing down on top of her. Kay, unhurt, a good
sport, laughed and the man on the ground with her laughed,
too. Kay was on her back, the football still clutched tightly
in her crooked arm. Dave Kelso was on his stomach, his
broad torso partially covering hers.

Fans in the stands were applauding. Teammates from
both sides were whistling and cheering. Kay and Dave lay on
the soft, well-tended carpet of grass, laughing uproariously, struggling to untangle arms and legs. When a shadow
fell between the giggling pair and the bright sun, Kay looked
up to see a livid Sullivan Ward above them.

Mouth thinned into a tight line, black eyes snapping,
Sullivan jerked her to her feet with such force and speed her
head rocked on her shoulders. Strong fingers possessively
gripping her arm, he was speaking to the blond Dave Kelso.
"What the hell do you think you're doing, Kelso?"

Still smiling, Dave Kelso rose, brushing grass and leaves
from his shorts. "Why so edgy, Ward? I didn't hurt her, did
I, sweetheart?" He looked down at Kay.

"He didn't, Sullivan, really. It was my fault, I should have...I was..."

Sullivan ignored her. "Kelso, this girl weighs a hundred pounds, you weigh two hundred. Fall on her again and you'll answer to me, you got that?"

"Meaning?"

"Read my lips, Kelso. Touch her again and I'll come after you. I weigh two hundred pounds, too."

The big blond man's smile stayed in place. "What if I took her out to dinner, Ward?" His eyes went to Kay. "I was just going to invite her when you interrupted."

Sullivan released Kay's arm. "You do that, Kelso." He turned to walk away. "On this playing field, stay off her!"

Kay, pulling her torn T-shirt together, apologized to the blond, good-natured man for the overreactive behavior of her morning-show partner. "Mr. Kelso, I'm sorry, Sullivan doesn't usually act so rudely."

"Kay." The smiling man took her arm and shook his blond head. "I've known Sullivan for over three years now and although he's not exactly a teddy bear, I've never seen him so mad. It can only mean one thing."

"I don't understand." Kay looked up at him.

"Don't you, Kay?" He chuckled easily. "And here I thought you were as intelligent as you are pretty."

Kay, riding back to the station after the game, a game in which Q102 had proved victorious, pondered the events of the morning. Sullivan was not in the limo she rode in. She had the distinct feeling that he had waited and watched to see what car she got into so that he might ride back in the other one.

The victors arrived back at the station. It had been arranged prior to the game that the losing team would treat the winners to beer and pizza at Leo's. Laughing, happy people piled out of the limo and headed directly across the street. Kay watched them go, promising she'd meet them there in ten minutes. In actuality, she had no intention of going to Leo's for the celebration. She wanted only to be

alone, to consider for herself why Sullivan had become so
angry when she'd tumbled to the ground with Dave.

Kay saw the other limo, the one Sullivan had taken back,
empty at the curb. Its occupants had already streamed across
Broadway and into the cozy pub. Surely Sullivan was by
now downing his first beer at Leo's. Kay alighted and went
into the Petroleum Club building and up to the studios.
They were deserted, save for the weekend substitute doing
his air trick. Kay was thankful for the privacy. She sighed
and started down the long hall to her office.

A loud noise stopped her.

The sound came from Sullivan's office. Kay switched
directions, moving quickly down the corridor to investi-
gate. Obviously thinking he was alone, Sullivan, his face
contorted, threw his other shoe across the room. It made the
same loud thud as the first one, which had drawn her attention. His back to her, he jerked his soiled white T-shirt over
his head and threw it after the shoes.

Kay stood watching his beautiful, bare back, sweat-slick
and shiny, lift with his breaths. Feeling her eyes on him at
last, he slowly turned around. Throat closing up, Kay swallowed. He started toward her and Kay could hear her
heartbeats in her ears. He looked for all the world like a
deadly predator stalking his helpless prey.

His eyes blazed with an undeniable look of passion that
both frightened and excited her. Feeling her knees turn to
water, Kay waited, eager for his strong arms to pull her to
him, longing for those lips to crush hers in a kiss of unrestrained hunger.

It never happened.

Stopping directly in front of her, Sullivan, his broad,
gleaming chest rising and falling rapidly, gained control of
himself and stopped what they both knew he'd intended.
For only a moment they stood toe to toe before he whirled
around, his back to her once again.

"Why aren't you at Leo's?" His voice was tired, flat.

"Why aren't you?" she responded softly.

His wide bare shoulders rose, then slowly fell. "Kay," he said, and it was a plea, "leave me alone. Please . . . please, leave me alone."

Four

———

That's exactly what Kay did. She left Sullivan alone. They did their morning show each day and during those four hours they were the only two people in all the world. Together they were on a madcap romp; laughing, teasing, flirting, dueling and enjoying every precious minute of it. The fact that every word they were saying was broadcast to an eager audience was often entirely forgotten by them. So the city of Denver and the state of Colorado were taken on the wild, exhilarating ride with the well-matched, charming, talented air personalities. The audience grew daily as word of mouth spread about the fascinating show. Once the newly informed had tuned in, they passed on the information to others. Sullivan, always good, was even better now that he had a delightful partner to play off.

The Sullivan-and-Kay show got better each and every day.

How shocked the audience would have been if they could have seen the change that took place when ten o'clock came each morning. As one turns off a spurting faucet, Sullivan would turn off the charm, rise from his chair and, without so much as a "see you later," depart for his office.

He grew colder, more aloof each day, and Kay was beginning to lose patience with him. It was nearing 5:00 p.m. on a day when chance had made her run into Sullivan three or four times in the course of the afternoon. Each of those times, he fixed her with that shuttered, arctic stare, and she'd grown increasingly angry with each encounter. She'd had just about enough of his uncivil treatment.

Fed up and furious, Kay stormed down the long corridor to Sullivan's office. Knocking loudly, she didn't wait to be invited in. She threw open the door, saying, "Sullivan Ward, I want—"

Sullivan shot up out of his chair. "If you don't mind, as you can see, I'm busy." He indicated a startled Janelle Davis, seated across from him, a steno pad on her lap.

"Janelle," Kay said sweetly, "I have to talk to Sullivan."

"Have you no manners, Kay?" Sullivan glared at her. "Sit down!" he commanded to a rising, nervous Janelle Davis.

"You're the one with bad manners, and I for one am sick of it!" Kay put her hands on her hips, looking defiantly at a seething Sullivan.

"I'm leaving," Janelle announced on her way out.

"Stay where you are, Janelle," Sullivan shouted angrily.

"You may go." Kay smiled sweetly, took Janelle's arm and escorted her to the door while a shocked Sullivan almost choked. Kay closed and locked the door and turned back to face him. "You sit down," she said commandingly, and watched the towering man slowly drop back down into his chair. "That's better," Kay said and circled his desk. She took a seat atop his desk, crossed her legs and said softly, "You and I need to have a little talk."

Kay saw the fury in the dark eyes and took a deep breath. Some of the fury subsided when he let them slowly slide from her face down to her legs. Well aware that the tight skirt she wore was riding up over her knees, Kay refused to pull it down. He was not going to make her nervous.

"Sullivan, you didn't want me back in Denver and I understand your reason." His eyes lifted to hers and he laced his long fingers across his stomach. He said nothing. "You were angry with me for leaving the show all those years ago. You thought me selfish and ambitious and perhaps you were right, but if you had—"

"I see nothing wrong with ambition," he interrupted coldly. "You stepped on me to climb one notch higher up the ladder. Well, that's fine, no hard feelings." Sullivan jerked a cigarette from a pack, lit it and added, "Certainly, there's no blame due you. If I, at age thirty-one, was fool enough to let a nineteen-year-old kid dump on me, well, shame on me."

"Sul ... it wasn't like that. It ... I—"

"It was exactly like that, Kay. I gave you a job as my partner against my better judgment. You were seventeen, the cutest little thing I'd ever seen, and you had talent. Nothing wrong with that. But I let you get under my skin and I wanted you." Sullivan pushed back his chair and rose, looking down at her. "Yeah, I wanted you so bad it drove me crazy and I told myself I was a fool, that you were a kid and I'd never forgive myself if I ..."

"Sul," Kay began, reached a hand out to him, but he caught it in midair.

"No, damn it, no. I don't want you touching me, can't you understand that?" His eyes were fierce again. "Can't we call it even? I broke the rules and made—I took you to bed, and for that I'm sorry. But you broke a few yourself, didn't you, sweetheart. You left me without so much as a goodbye."

Near tears, Kay said breathlessly, "Oh, Sul, I didn't want to, but you—"

He looked disgusted. "Sure, sure. You had no choice. I'm tired of reminiscing, Kay. I really have got work to do, so if you'll just leave ..."

Beaten, Kay slid from his desk. "Fine, you refuse to listen. I'll not try to explain further, but do me a favor, will you?"

Sullivan looked down at her. Her face wore a pleading look that tore him apart. "What, Kay?" he said evenly.

"Can't we put the past behind us? Won't you be my friend, or if not a friend, at least will you stop hating me? I'll leave you alone, Sullivan, but there are times we have to be together, you know that. Am I asking for the moon?"

Muscles tensing, black eyes softening, Sullivan, silently thinking he would give her the moon with a bow around it if it would make her love him the way he loved her, said softly, "No, Kay, you're not. I've been a bastard, I know it, and I'm sorry. You're right, the past is dead. There's no reason we can't get along like two responsible adults. Forgive me?"

"I'd forgive you anything," she said. Sullivan felt his heart speed out of control.

Calmly he smiled. "You're a good kid, Kay."

"Sullivan," she reminded him softly, "the kid you knew is gone. I'm a woman."

"I stand corrected." He grinned down at her.

Autumn came and with it the turning of the aspen. Kay was eager to drive up into the mountains to see nature's glorious display, so when Sullivan informed her that she, Jeff and he had been engaged to broadcast live from a new condominium project up in the lovely little hamlet of Evergreen, Kay was delighted.

On a clear, perfect fall day near the end of September, Kay, wedged in between Sullivan and Jeff, rode in the rear seat of the Q102 remote rig up the winding road to Evergreen. The chief engineer was at the wheel. Blazing color as far as the eye could see made Kay smile and point. She felt wonderfully alive and happy to be back in her home state.

"How are your parents liking Florida?" Jeff sipped from a mug of coffee.

"Mom loves it, Dad misses Colorado," Kay said, her eyes still darting out the windows to look at the beauty surrounding them. "I think if they hadn't sold their home here, he'd consider moving back."

"Nope," Jeff said resolutely, "they wouldn't."

"Why do you say that?" Kay looked at him, puzzled.

"You just said, 'Mom loves Florida.' Don't women always get their way?" His eyes twinkled and Kay poked him in the ribs with an elbow. She turned back to look out once more.

"Oh, there," she said, smiling happily, "a doe. A baby doe." She leaned across Sullivan to get a better look. "See, isn't it adorable?" Realizing suddenly that she was draping herself across him, Kay looked up at his face and said hastily, "I'm sorry I..."

To her shocked amazement, he grinned easily and said, "The doe is cute. So vulnerable."

"Yes," Kay agreed, and straightened.

The remote broadcast at the site of the new half-timbered condos went well. The three air personalities, doing a live radio remote from inside the compact studio on wheels, drew a big crowd. There was never a minute when admiring fans weren't standing in front of the glass-enclosed truck, waving to the three. The real-estate promoters were delighted. Lookers turned out en masse and by the time the broadcast ended at two in the afternoon, several contracts had been written up on new, expensive condos.

After the sign off Jeff, dressed in his favorite garb—frayed cutoffs, a white sweatshirt and a black-billed cap with the gold braid denoting captain—suggested they have lunch before driving back down to Denver. Sullivan and Kay, both starving, quickly agreed.

At a sunny sidewalk café in the artsy little community, Kay, Sullivan and Jeff sat at a small table covered with a red-checkered cloth. Full and lazy after eating huge corned-beef sandwiches and plates of potato salad, the three lounged listlessly in the near-deserted little outdoor restaurant, relaxed, content, enjoying the beautiful autumn day.

Kay, stealing glances at Sullivan, smiled as he told Jeff excitedly of his plans for future promotions. His ebony hair was disheveled and gleaming in the afternoon sun, his navy windbreaker unzipped, revealing a close-fitting shirt of canary yellow. He looked boyishly handsome as he moved his arms around, describing how he envisioned the Columbus

Day parade. Kay hardly heard his plans. She was too busy drinking in his masculine beauty, the way his hands moved through the air as he talked, the fire flashing in the black eyes, the mobile mouth stretched into a grin, exposing dazzling white teeth in a dark, handsome face.

"Exactly." Sullivan pounded the table for emphasis and reached out for another cigarette. He felt in his pocket for a match. "Give me a light, will you, Jeff?"

Jeff, absently turning a match pack over and over in his right hand, flipped it to Sullivan. "By the way—" Jeff's eyes began to twinkle with mischief "—what ever happened to that gold lighter you always carried? You lose it?" Jeff could hardly suppress his teasing laughter. He had a very good idea what had happened to the lighter his old friend had valued for so long.

Kay watched as steady brown hands lit the cigarette and flipped the matches back to Jeff. Sullivan, his face devoid of expression, said calmly, "A long time ago."

Sullivan's changed attitude made life more pleasant for Kay. And for everyone else who came in contact with him. Kay surmised he'd finally decided to let bygones be bygones. He was like the Sullivan she'd met all those years ago: congenial, patient, but holding her at arm's length.

Kay became relaxed around him and hurried in and out of his office with ideas just as she'd done when she was a starry-eyed kid eager for advice and praise from her knowledgeable mentor. Sullivan was never too busy to listen, to make suggestions, to offer help.

Kay, working late on Friday evening, swiveled around in her chair, rubbed her tired eyes and decided it was time to leave. Rapidly cleaning off her desk, she locked her office and started toward the lobby. At the end of the corridor, Sullivan's door stood open, though there were no lights burning inside.

She started grinning.

Without qualms, she strolled into his office, tossed her handbag onto the leather couch and looked up at the high chinning bar. She'd been dying to try it since the day she returned. She could recall so vividly Sullivan showing her how to chin herself and the two of them breaking up with laughter over her awkwardness. When finally she'd managed the feat, she'd been rewarded with warm, loving kisses from the laughing man standing below her.

Kay kicked off her shoes, smoothed her hands on the skirt of her dove-gray dress and walked to the bar. Tossing back her head, she lifted her arms high in the air toward the steel cylinder. Biting her lip, she lunged up and her fingertips touched the shiny bar. Standing on tiptoe, Kay stretched as high as possible and managed after a couple of failed attempts to wrap her fingers tightly around the bar. She did it underhanded, just as she'd been instructed.

With a little gasp of victory, she laboriously lifted herself up until she was able to press her lifted chin over the cylinder. Face flushed, stockinged feet swinging in midair, Kay giggled happily. Deep male laughter joined tinkling female laughter.

Startled, Kay's laughter subsided as her surprised gaze went to the man lounging in the doorway. "Very good." Sullivan chuckled and started toward her.

Kay, clinging to the bar, froze, speechless, and watched him nearing her. He stopped directly in front of her and slowly wrapped his long arms around her hips. "Sullivan, I can get down by—"

"Release the bar, Kay," he said, the warm smile still on his upturned face.

Kay did. She moved her chin back and uncurled her fingers, letting her hands go to the tops of Sullivan's wide shoulders. Laughing again, she said, "Guess it's a good thing you came by. I might have hung up there all night."

"Yeah," he said softly. For a time he held her there, his arms folded tightly beneath her bottom. Kay, her pelvis resting against his hard chest, hands on his shoulders, saw the laughter leaving the dark eyes.

Slowly, carefully, Sullivan let her slide downward, never releasing his hold on her. Their eyes locked. She felt her body moving sinuously down his, felt the tight skirt sliding up, up, even as she slid down. Neither spoke. Her stockinged feet were touching the floor now, but her hands remained on his shoulders and his hands were on her hips. They stood pressed closely together, the hem of her skirt bunched up against his hard thighs.

They stood in the rapidly darkening room, high above the city, looking at each other, neither daring to breathe, to move. Senses reeling, Kay was acutely aware of the warm, granite-hard body touching hers from chest to toes. The roughness of the denim encasing his long, muscular legs was pleasantly ticklish to her thighs, which were protected only by silky pantyhose.

Instinctively pressing closer to his tall, powerful body, Kay gloried in the feel of his virile masculinity. When she opened her eyes to look at him once more, his dark gaze had gone to her hair. A big hand moved up to cradle her head tenderly while his eyes eagerly caressed the long, shiny hair.

"You know," he said in that velvet voice that warmed her so, "Jeff's wrong."

Kay licked dry lips with the tip of her tongue. "About what?"

That intense black gaze still on her hair, he said musingly, "He says your hair looks like a Christmas angel, but it doesn't." Long fingers gently raked through silky locks. "It's more like captured moonlight, shimmering and silvery and breathtaking." His eyes slid back to hers and his head slowly descended. Kay sighed. Sullivan softly kissed the left corner of Kay's mouth.

His lips lifted immediately from hers. Kay felt his hands move. She waited. Her lips parted expectantly, her hands tightened on his shoulders, her pulse raced with anticipation.

Sullivan gently set her back a step and, looking only at her upturned face, he chivalrously lowered her skirt down over her thighs. Kay's fingers gripped at his neck and she said, "But, Sul, please don't . . ."

"I don't intend to," he said, plucking her fingers from his neck. "But I can't stand here with you in my arms and your dress pushed up to your gorgeous bottom without wanting to." He smiled at her, turned and strolled casually away.

"Night, Kay," he said over his shoulder and left a stunned Kay looking after him. Trembling with need, Kay jammed a hand to her mouth to quell the sobs of frustration threatening to erupt from her tight throat.

Through the darkened reception area, Sullivan Ward took long strides, anxious to get outside and away from the silver-haired temptation. Heart pounding, jaw flexing, abdomen tautened and aching, Sullivan gulped at the fresh night air when he stepped outside. Groaning with relief when he reached his gray Mercedes, Sullivan couldn't resist. He tilted his dark head back and looked up, counting the windows across to the corner office where he'd left her.

A shudder shook his long, lean body and he jerked open the car door, lunged into the seat and sped away as though a modern-day Lorelei was seductively urging him to the fatal rocks.

"Kay." It was Janelle Davis's soft voice. "If you aren't too busy, could I come by your office and speak to you about your costume for the Columbus Day parade?"

It was shortly before noon on Monday. "Of course you can, Janelle. In fact, I'm getting hungry. Why don't you and I grab a salad or a sandwich together?"

"Sure, all right. That would be nice," Janelle responded.

Half an hour later the two women sat at the Café Promenade in Larimer Square, the beautifully restored older part of downtown Denver. A favorite of the tourists, historic Larimer Square gave the visitor a feel of Denver's colorful past. Kay loved the place.

Janelle Davis daintily sliced a piece of cheese on the carved cheese board, took a tiny bite, smiled and said, "Just delicious."

Kay sipped her wine and nodded. "Sullivan tells me the theme of this year's parade is to be the old west."

"Yes, I think it will be great fun." Janelle smiled and confided, "Sullivan's going to ride a beautiful black horse."

"Good Lord." Kay's eyes clouded. "I won't be expected to ride, will I?"

"Oh, no, certainly not. Sullivan said you'll ride on the Q102 float."

"Whew." Kay grinned. "That's a load off. I'm scared to death of horses."

"Yes, I know."

"You do?" Kay's silver brows lifted.

"Well, yes, Sullivan mentioned it. He also mentioned what he'd like you to wear in the parade."

"Oh?"

"Yes, he said he thought it would be appropriate if you'd be the schoolmarm."

"No."

"No?" Janelle patted at her mouth with a linen napkin, her gray eyes filled with surprise.

"No, Janelle, I don't want to dress like a schoolmarm; that would be as dull as dishwater." Kay smiled. "My crafty partner. He's to make a grand, dashing figure atop a coal-black stallion while little Miss Clark sits on a float, hands folded in her lap, dressed in a white blouse, long skirt and hair in a bun at the back of her head."

"I don't see it that way, Kay, but perhaps, if you'd like, you could dress up as Annie Oakley." Janelle looked at Kay expectantly.

"Was Annie Oakley Sullivan's idea, too?"

Janelle's face reddened. "Yes. He said you might not like the schoolmarm idea, so...."

"He's so right, nor do I intend to be Annie Oakley. Order me a costume of a hurdy-gurdy girl. You know, a dance-hall dress. I'd like a flamboyant eye-catching satin outfit with mesh hose and a feathered hat and... What? What's wrong?"

Janelle, an expression of displeasure on her face, was shaking her head. "Kay, you just can't do that."

"Oh, yes, I can." Kay leaned forward. "Look, Janelle, I may work for Sullivan, but I'm no child, to be told what I can and cannot do. Did Sullivan tell the rest of the air personalities what to wear?"

"That's different, Kay."

Kay frowned. "Why? Because I'm a woman? Because I'm some airhead incapable of making decisions for myself? Because he's older than me and thinks I'm still a kid?" Kay was growing angry.

"That's unfair, Kay. Sullivan just—"

"Janelle, you're a very nice lady, but you're too damned protective of Sullivan!"

"Yes, I suppose I am," Janelle admitted sadly. "Just as Sullivan is overly protective of you."

"Janelle, I'm sorry. I know that—"

"Don't be. Sullivan has never thought of me as anything other than a friend. If you didn't exist, that would still be the case. But I'll tell you something, Kay, hurt him and I'll snatch you bald headed."

Kay smiled and touched Janelle's hand. "I like you, Janelle Davis."

"Same here." Janelle grinned.

"Order me that dance-hall costume and don't say a word to Sullivan."

"I will and I won't."

Bright October sunlight caused Kay to open her eyes and blink. She knew before she looked at the clock that she'd overslept. Groaning, Kay tossed back the covers, took a quick shower and pulled on her jeans and a sweatshirt.

The Columbus Day parade was to begin promptly at ten o'clock. The city fathers had decided to have the parade on the Saturday before the actual holiday to insure a good turnout. Kay, used to rising early every morning, hadn't set her alarm, certain she'd awake with time to spare.

Now, at five after nine, she was speeding toward the station in her red Porsche, wondering how she'd ever be able to get dressed and down to the corner of Fifteenth and Golden, where the Q102 float would be waiting. Kay roared into the parking lot and scurried into the station. Panting for breath, she went to her office and saw a note taped to the door.

"Kay, your costume is in Sullivan's office. Janelle."

Kay turned and sped down the hall. The station was quiet. Save the weekend deejay doing his air trick, no one was around. All the other participants were either already at the parade site or else across the street at Leo's, having champagne mixed with orange juice. Kay threw open the door to Sullivan's office and saw a big box resting on the couch. She opened it and drew out a shiny green-satin dress, a pair of black mesh hose, a green-satin garter, a pair of very high heels, and a green-satin hat with a curling green feather.

Kay smiled, slammed the office door closed and picked up the shiny dress. She held it up to her slender frame and winced when she saw how low the strapless costume dipped in front. Shrugging her shoulders, Kay lifted the sweatshirt over her head and unzipped her jeans.

Rushing as much as possible, she soon stood frowning before the big mirror. Mesh hose and high heels on, satin hat pinned atop her upswept hair, its feather curving seductively over her ear and down under her chin, Kay was frantically trying to hook up the back of the tight dress. Arms bent behind her, she fumbled with the stubborn hooks and looked at herself, her cheeks staining a bright red.

Her high breasts were practically spilling from the snug bodice. The full skirt reached her knees, but the hem was folded back over the dress at one point, showing off white, frilly ruffles as well as a long, stockinged leg. The green garter was visible upon her left thigh. Momentarily wishing she'd been less pigheaded and had dressed as a schoolmarm, Kay gasped when the office door opened.

In the portal a tall, dark cowboy stood gaping at her. Booted feet apart, the intruder's black eyes flashed with menace. A tailored shirt of snowy white stretched across muscular shoulders; a star of shiny silver flashed upon his chest. Tight black trousers revealed the lean, hard muscles of his thighs. Around his narrow hips, a gun belt of smooth leather rode low, a silver pistol in the holster. Upon his head a pearl-gray Stetson was pulled low, and on his hands, gloves of soft black kid leather fit like a second skin.

"Sullivan!" she gasped, clutching frantically at her open dress, her wide blue eyes fastened on his tall frame filling the door.

Sullivan lifted a hand upward. With an index finger he pushed the brim of his low-riding hat to the back of his head, releasing a shock of black hair. He looked angry.

His dark eyes raking over her, Sullivan shook his head and took a step inside, closing the door behind him. Kay unwaveringly met his furious gaze, although her stomach was doing a flip-flop and the hands at the back of her gaping dress began to tremble.

Kay lifted her chin and said commandingly, "Sullivan, could you help me fasten my costume? I'm having a little trouble with the hooks." She smiled sweetly at him as though she'd not noticed his displeasure. Sullivan stood looking at the vision in green standing before him. Torn between the urge to spank her soundly for choosing such a daring costume and the almost uncontrollable desire to let his hands run all over the exposed soft flesh, he stood glaring at her. Refusing to let him get the best of her, Kay continued to smile and said calmly, "Are you going to help me, Sullivan?"

Sullivan couldn't keep from smiling back. Rigid body relaxing, he started to her. "I'm not Sullivan. I'm the marshal, ma'am, and I ought to arrest you for going about half-naked."

Relief flooding her body, Kay laughed and took up the game. "Oh, marshal, please don't take me to jail. I'll be plenty decent just as soon as this dress is hooked up." She batted long silky eyelashes at him.

"I doubt that." He grinned, his eyes moving to the swell of her breasts. "But I'll do what I can." He pulled off his black leather gloves, stuffed them into a hip pocket and came to stand behind her. Nimble brown fingers went to the tiny hooks at the waist of the green-satin getup. "Move your hands, Kay, and I'll have this taken care of in a minute."

"I'm all yours," she said, smiling. Her eyes went to the mirror across from them. She stood directly in front of the tall, handsome Sullivan. His dark head, the Stetson pushed back, was bent a little, his eyes on the task at hand. He was completely absorbed. Or so Kay thought.

Kay felt warm hands brushing the bare skin of her back as Sullivan tugged at the tiny hooks. A shiver went up her spine. She wondered if he felt it. He continued to work doggedly, managing to close only two or three of the closely spaced fastenings. All at once the big hands stilled, his head raised and his eyes slid slowly from her exposed back up to the fragile column of her neck.

Wordlessly, his hands left the dress and gently cupped her bare shoulders. Turning his head, he lowered his lips to her nape, kissing her lightly. Sullivan raised his head. He looked at her in the mirror and said softly, his lips near her ear, "What am I doing dressing you when all I've ever wanted to do is undress you?"

Kay opened her mouth, but no words would come. A little gasp escaped her lips and Sullivan pulled her gently back against his tall, hard body. He lifted a hand to push aside the ticklish feather of her hat and pressed his open lips to the sensitive cord going down her neck.

"Sul, oh, Sul," Kay whispered breathlessly, tilting her head to give him total access.

"Kay," he murmured hoarsely, while he nibbled tenderly. "Why do you have to be so sweet, so clean." His tongue teased at the tender spot beneath her ear. "Why must I feel I'll starve without the taste of you?"

Kay sighed and turned her face toward his. Sullivan's lips lifted and he looked into her shining blue eyes. He moaned and slowly lowered his mouth to her soft, parted lips. He kissed her with restrained passion, trying desperately to control the fire she'd kindled in him. He might have been able to repress the raging desire just below the surface, if not for the fact that when their lips separated, his eyes dropped downward just as one side of the low-cut green dress revealed to his heated gaze a brief, fleeting glimpse of the rosy-hued crest of a creamy white breast.

It was his total undoing.

Sullivan groaned, pulled her back against him once again and let his hands slide up her rib cage to the top of the dress. With his lips in her hair and his deep, drugging voice whispering her name, he slowly peeled the green satin down to her waist. Kay didn't protest.

She pressed her head back against his shoulder and trembled, unable to fight what was happening to him, to her. She closed her eyes and savored the feel of those strong, smooth hands spreading warmly on her now bare midriff. With a gentleness that left her breathless, those sure hands moved up her trembling body, tenderly cupping her bare breasts.

Unbelievable warmth and pleasure quickly flooded Kay's being. Her breasts swelled to fill his hands, and when his thumbs brushed at their aching peaks, she said his name softly. Her eyes remained closed, her face turning to press into the warmth of his throat. Open-mouthed, she kissed his smooth cheek, licking a line along his chiseled jawline with her tongue.

"Kay." His voice was husky. "Kay, honey, open your eyes."

Face still turned, she let her eyes open and gasped when she cut them across the room toward the mirror. "Sul," she bit her lip and once again closed her eyes.

"No, sweet baby," he pleaded. "Open your eyes and look. Look at us, honey. You're beautiful, God, you're so beautiful."

Face flushed, Kay opened her eyes again. In the mirror two eager lovers were caught and framed. At Sullivan's soft urgings, she let her embarrassment slip away and watched with unabashed pleasure as the hands of the only man she'd ever loved gently, expertly caressed her naked breasts, driving her slowly, happily insane. "Sullivan. We are…oh, Sul, kiss me. Please."

Sullivan's hands reluctantly left her breasts; he turned her in his arms and pulled her up against his tall, hard body. His mouth lowered to hers and all restraint was gone. Hungrily, deeply he kissed her, holding her head in his spread fingers to press her closer. Sighing into his mouth, Kay pushed the Stetson from his head and ran an eager hand up into his thick, black hair, her senses reeling from the heated mouth devouring hers, the smoky taste of his lips and tongue so familiar, so strange.

Kay was vaguely aware of something on Sullivan's broad chest pressing into her naked shoulder. It was mildly abrasive, nothing more, and it was forgotten when his hot, wet tongue dipped deeper into her mouth to expertly, tantalizingly sweep and taste every tingling part, finally drawing her tongue into his mouth.

Weak, dizzy, thrumming with desire, Kay clung to him, loving the feel of his mouth feasting on hers, his hands moving up and down over her bare back and finally sliding over her satin-clad hips to press her ever closer to the pulsing, throbbing hardness straining against his tight black trousers.

His mouth slid from hers and went to her chin. "No woman in this world kisses me the way my sweet baby does," he said. "You know just what I like, don't you honey?"

"I...yes, yes, Sul," she murmured, her heart pounding with happiness and hunger.

His mouth, hot and moist, was nibbling at her throat while he called her name and moaned. That persuasive mouth began to move lower and Sullivan muttered thickly, "I want to kiss you all over, Kay, all over... Every sweet part of you."

Kay couldn't answer. Eyes closing in ecstasy, her hands were once again in the thick, dark hair of his head, unconsciously urging his mouth down toward the bare, swelling breasts, aching for his touch. Her eyes fluttered open just as his mouth closed over a pale crest in a warm caress that made her shudder.

Lips upon the hard little peak, Sullivan murmured, "Sweet. Oh, God, so very sweet."

"Hey, Ward." Jeff Kern's voice was followed by a pounding knock on the door.

"Sullivan!" Kay gasped, horrified.

Sullivan, eyes still glazed with passion, stepped protectively in front of Kay, shielding her should Jeff open the

door. "Be right with you, Jeffrey." His voice was just a bit
shaky. "Stay where you are, we're on our way out." Broad
chest rising and falling rapidly, muscles bunching in his jaw,
Sullivan deftly hooked up the green-satin dress, while Kay,
trembling, stood docilely in front of him.

"All done," he whispered and she turned to face him.
Sullivan winced. There on her delicate white shoulder, red
blotches from the punishing silver star on his chest looked
tender and raw. "Kay, I'm sorry," he said, and Kay knew
he was apologizing for more than chapped flesh. Before she
could respond, he retrieved his Stetson from the floor,
jerked a coiled lariat from atop his desk and hurried her to
the door.

Jeff Kerns, dressed as a piano player in an old-time
sporting house, stood with his arms folded over his chest. "I
was beginning to..." His words trailed off as he looked from
Sullivan to Kay and back again. Eyes twinkling devilishly,
his lips began lifting into a pleased smile.

"Open your mouth and I'll shut it for you, Jeffrey." Sullivan glared down at him. Jeff remained silent, but he lifted
a hand to his mouth and with thumb and forefinger pan-
tomimed zipping his lips while he winked at Kay. She
couldn't keep from smiling.

Jeff took her elbow, made a face at Sullivan and said to
her in a stage whisper, "Let's ignore him and perhaps he'll
disappear." He glanced back over his shoulder at the tall
man cupping his hands to light a cigarette. To Kay, Jeff
continued, his eyes dancing, "He's got the shakes so bad
he's either had too much coffee or not enough of—"

"Can it, Jeff," barked a frustrated Sullivan Ward.

The Columbus Day parade was a crowd-pleasing, spectacular success. Marching bands from across the state,
equestrian units, huge flower-laden floats, precision drill
teams and unicycle-riding clowns all drew applause from the
people lining the parade route.

The Q102 float was positioned near the very end of the
procession. It was fortunate, since Sullivan, Kay and Jeff
were late arriving and the first bands and floats were al-

ready making slow, steady progress up Fifteenth Street. Janelle Davis, her high forehead creased with worry, saw Sullivan towering above the crowd, gave a sigh of relief then opened her mouth to berate him for his tardiness.

"Sullivan Ward, why on..." Her voice trailed away when she saw Kay, then Jeff.

"Not now, Janelle," Sullivan said harshly.

"Better not rattle his cage," Jeff Kerns lightheartedly informed her while Sullivan wordlessly left the others and strode determinedly to where his saddled black horse was waiting. "Right, Kay?"

Kay, her lips slightly swollen from Sullivan's heated kisses, her face still flushed, knees weak, said diplomatically, "It's my fault we're late, Janelle, really. I was in my costume...Sullivan gave me a hand."

"I see." Janelle's gray eyes held a knowing look.

"Sure he didn't give you a couple?" Jeff quipped.

"A couple of what?" Kay chewed her lip.

"Hands, darlin'," Jeff kidded and lifted her up onto the high float where the rest of the Q102 air personalities were in position.

At a circular green-felt table, Dale Kitrell, Dallas Smith, Ace Black and one of the salespeople sat playing cards, stacks of colored chips in front of them, shot glasses filled with weak tea at their elbows. Sherry Jones, garbed in a long blue brocade dress, a black feather boa wrapped around her throat and falling to the floor down her back, was the dealer. Happy and laughing, her hair gleamed as she tossed her head around, enjoying immensely all the attention.

At a polished mahogany bar, the plump, muttonchopped bartender was Sam Shults. Smiling warmly at Kay, he wiped an already sparkling glass. Jeff lifted Kay atop the bar. "By the way," Jeff said, close to her ear, "did Sullivan think to mention that he is supposed to ride by, rope you and—"

"No!" Kay hoped he was teasing.

"I'm getting worried about Ward. He's mighty forgetful lately." He tweaked his false mustache, patted her hand and added, "If you see him riding up, you're to helpfully raise your arms above your head, okay?"

"But Jeff—" she gritted her teeth.

"Not my idea." He shrugged merrily, snapped the arm garters around his elbows and took his seat at the old upright player piano.

Kay, her legs crossed, sat atop the bar and waved to the onlookers. Her daring outfit drew catcalls and whistles and she colored and wished for the second time this day that she'd dressed more modestly. The crowd fully approved of her glittering green garb and called her name and ran up to the slow traveling float to get her autograph, to touch her hand, to tell her how much they enjoyed the Sullivan and Kay morning show.

Gracious, she smiled and waved and posed prettily, and all the while she was thinking of what had happened just prior to the parade. It was all she could do to keep from lifting her fingers to touch her lips, as though the imprint of Sullivan's masterful mouth would still be there. Invisible though it was, his brand was on her. It had been from the very first time he'd ever kissed her.

There'd been men in her life in California; some handsome, some charming and extremely entertaining. She'd shared kisses with a couple that had made her heart speed pleasantly, but Sullivan Ward was the only man for her. There'd never been another lover, never. That one passionate night together had meant too much, had been too beautiful. She'd been a virgin when Sullivan had so tenderly taken her on that never-to-be-forgotten night. With his intimate possession of her willing, innocent body, he'd become the holder of her heart.

Now he'd again aroused in her the raging passions he'd introduced all those years ago. There'd been times when she'd almost forgotten what it was like to be held by Sullivan, kissed by him. There in his office on this perfect fall day, he'd kissed her with that old urgent fire, looked at her with that dark smoldering gaze, pressed her to his hard male body and made her weak with love and wanting.

"Hey, Sullivan." Someone shouting his name snapped Kay's head around. "Why isn't your partner riding with you?"

Kay's eyes went to the commanding figure regally sitting on a huge black horse, as Sullivan advanced on the slow-moving float. Kay swallowed and clutched at the polished saloon bar, her wide eyes on dark horse and dark rider.

Hat tilted strategically low over one eye, white teeth flashing, Sullivan easily reined the prancing, silver-embellished black stallion along the slippery pavement, moving steadily closer. To the waving, admiring crowd, he shouted in that deep, melodious voice, "You know, I think my pretty partner should be with me at all times." His eyes gleamed devilishly and Kay colored, reading a personal meaning into his careless words.

Sullivan pulled the horse up, draped a white-sleeved forearm over the saddle horn and with a slow turn of his head, directed his attention, and that of the crowd, to a nervous, smiling Kay.

When Sullivan winked and tipped his hat to the crowd, straightened in the saddle and unhooked a coiled lariat from its resting place, the crowd went wild.

Showboating grandly, Sullivan let the coiled rope slide down over a bent arm, drew a cigarette from his shirt pocket, lit it and exhaled. Kay, along with everyone else, had eyes only for the compelling man so easily, expertly playing his role.

"Yup," he drawled dramatically, "I think that little filly belongs in the custody of the marshal, just for being so danged brazenly beautiful. Don't ya'll?"

Loud, urging applause and piercing whistles were his answer.

Clamping his cigarette firmly between his teeth, Sullivan nodded, wrapped the reins around the horn and knee-reined his big, well-trained stallion toward the Q102 float and Kay. He uncoiled the rope, made a large loop and began twirling it high over his head. All the while, he looked directly at Kay; cigarette smoke drifting up into his dark, squinting eyes.

Kay, as impressed with his performance as was the cheering crowd, completely forgot about lifting her arms over her head. Heart racing rapidly, she was torn between the urgent desire to be held close to Sullivan and the fear she had of horses. She sat frozen in place, green dress glittering, mesh-hosed legs crossed, silver hair shining in the unfiltered rays of the Colorado sun.

When a perfectly thrown rope fell over her head and tightened as soon as it reached her waist, Kay blinked and winced. Arms pinned to her sides, she felt as helpless as a trapped butterfly. Sullivan urged his horse closer, lithely stood in the saddle, and in one fast, fluid movement, plucked Kay from the saloon bar.

Someone softly screamed and Kay realized it must have been her when Sullivan, tossing his half-smoked cigarette away, gently pressed her back against his chest and said softly into her ear, "Don't be afraid, Kay. I'd never let you fall."

Five

Sullivan didn't let Kay fall, but he sure did let her down. The parade continued and she sat across the saddle in front of him. Kay was happy, hopeful, unafraid. Sullivan, after deftly removing the rope, held Kay in his arms while they rode the prancing horse down the street.

Kay forgot her fear of horses and waved gaily to the cheering crowd. How could she be frightened; the man she loved was holding her in his protective arms.

The dazzling smiles she gave the crowd reflected the bubbling happiness inside. Kay was sure that as soon as the parade ended, as soon as she and Sullivan could be alone...

Stomach fluttering, eyes sparkling, Kay, female that she was, mentally planned what she would wear on this evening of evenings. There was no doubt in her mind that Sullivan would want to take her out to dinner or to come to her place for a meal. Good Lord, she had nothing to feed him. Nothing. She'd have to run by the supermarket and choose a couple of rib eyes, some ingredients for the salad, potatoes for baking. Sullivan could bring the wine.

She could wear the new blue loose-knit sweater and suede skirt if they had dinner at her place; if he wanted to go out, she'd wear the daring netted V-backed black silk. It was sexy and elegant and Sullivan was sure to like it.

Heart full of love, head full of plans, Kay's warm eyes left the spectators, lifting almost shyly to look at Sullivan. His gaze was resting on the red, blotchy flesh of her white shoulder and his jaw was set, though he wore a smile.

"Don't worry about it," she whispered gaily. "It's only a small abrasion."

His eyes flicked up to hers, but he said nothing. It was Kay's first warning that things were not going to be as wonderful as she'd thought.

The parade came to its conclusion at the far end of Broadway. There, Janelle Davis, behind the wheel of Sullivan's gray Mercedes, waited to drive Sullivan, Kay and Jeff back to the station.

Kay was stunned when Sullivan, after helping her down from the horse, turned the mount over to a waiting stable boy and walked to the car. Wordlessly, he climbed into the front passenger seat, leaving her standing.

A warm hand gripped her elbow and Jeff's familiar voice said, "I see ole 'strong and silent' is cranky again." He laughed, walked Kay to the Mercedes and handed her inside, following her.

Janelle, turning to smile and speak to Kay and Jeff, gasped and asked bluntly, "Kay. Your shoulder! It's all pink and raw. What happened to you?"

Kay, her face turning as pink as the punished shoulder, said evenly, "I suppose it's some sort of allergy." Sullivan, his long arm draped along the car seat, gritted his teeth as his hand tightened on the plush upholstery.

Jeff hit Sullivan's shoulder and said wickedly, "Yeah, she's either allergic to horses or to Sullivan, and I've never seen a horse that..."

A dark head swung around and Sullivan fixed Jeff with a hard stare. "Your stale humor may go over with your listeners, but I find it offensive. I told you earlier, shut your damned mouth or I'll do it for you." Sullivan turned back around, moved his arm from the seat and lit a cigarette.

Unruffled, Jeff winked at Kay and laughed. Janelle, shaking her head, drove back to the radio station and Kay, confused, uneasy, thought that surely when they arrived, she'd get the chance to speak to Sullivan alone.

It was not to be.

To her shock, Sullivan slid under the wheel as soon as Janelle got out. "I'll see you guys later," he said, and before Kay, standing numbly beside the car, could speak, he'd driven away.

"There goes a real jerk," Jeff said, laughing, and put his arms around Kay and Janelle. He added, "Let's all go over to Leo's and drown our troubles. What do you say?"

Both women declined.

By the time Kay had changed back into her jeans and was driving home to her apartment, the bright sunshine had departed. Ominous clouds now blanketed the city and the temperature was rapidly dropping. A cold winter rain was beginning when Kay pulled the red Porsche into the underground garage below her apartment building.

Kay stepped into her dim living room, tossed her bag and car keys on the marble-topped table in the entranceway and sighed. Not bothering to turn on any lamps, she went directly to the long white sofa and stretched out wearily, hands folded beneath her head.

She stayed there for the rest of the long, dreary afternoon. Hurt and disappointed, she felt lifeless, unable to move. She could only lie there, prone, puzzling over Sullivan's mercurial moods. How could he be so passionate and loving one minute, so cold and uncaring the next?

All afternoon, Kay's unhappy eyes kept going to the silent telephone. Why didn't he call? Why didn't he come over? Why did he torment her so?

It was dark, though Kay had no idea what time it was, when she went to her closet and pulled out a raincoat. The windshield wipers made an irritating sound as Kay drove across town. The swish-swish of the rubber-bladed wipers grated on already raw nerves.

Kay wheeled into the only space in front of the elegant Park Lane Towers, parked and jumped out of the car. Rain brushed her face as she ran up the steps to the opulent lobby. Kay put a charming smile on her face when the uniformed doorman saw her, and she pointed upward, then shrugged slender shoulders as though she'd lost her key.

The man nodded knowingly and threw open the heavy glass door. Kay rushed inside, relieved. If she'd had to ring the buzzer of Sullivan's apartment, she was not at all sure he'd have let her in the front door. "So sorry," Kay said to the doorman, "I was sure my key was in my handbag." She hurried to the elevator before he could answer.

Kay stood, drenched, shaking and wondering what had possessed her. She was on the nineteenth floor, just outside the door of Sullivan's penthouse apartment. She gulped for air, squared her shoulders and knocked decisively.

"Yeah, it's open," came the irascible male voice.

Kay cringed and thought of fleeing. Cold hand on the shiny brass knob, she turned, pushed in the heavy door and stepped inside. Slowly she closed it behind her.

It was dark in the big room. Only one light burned and it was an elbow lamp casting its concentrated circular disk of illumination on the glass-topped table where it rested. A half-full bottle of Scotch sat beneath the lamp. A glass of the amber liquid sat beside the bottle. A dark hand slowly moved from the darkness to curl its fingers around the glass.

A faceless voice from the shadows said coldly, "Is there something you need?"

"Yes," Kay said resolutely, and shrugged out of her wet raincoat and hung it on a brass coat tree. She turned, pulled nervously at the bottom of her blue sweater, descended the three steps leading into the big pine-paneled room and walked toward the light.

Sullivan remained where he was, saying nothing, lifting the Scotch to his lips. He lounged lazily in a leather easy chair. One long leg was hooked over the chair's arm, the other stretched in front of him, resting on a matching leather ottoman. He wore no shoes, no shirt.

Kay stood above him, straining to see. "Can I offer you a drink?" came the faceless voice. "There's ice in the..."

"I don't want a drink, Sullivan." Kay warily took a seat on the big soft ottoman beside his bare foot. "And I wish that you wouldn't drink, either."

Sullivan leaned slowly up into the light. His hair was disheveled and his beard was beginning to grow. He looked menacing. Possessively clasping the bottle of Scotch, he warned, "If you've any foolish ideas about being some kind of junior Carrie Nation with breaking bottles of liquor in mind, forget it. This is the only bottle I have and I plan to drink it."

"It's not like you to drink, Sullivan."

"How the hell do you know what's like me?"

Kay looked into his angry dark eyes. Their gazes held for a minute; then Sullivan leaned back into the darkness once again. "You never used to drink, Sul."

"My name is Sullivan. Stop calling me Sul." He lifted the glass to his lips.

"I'm sorry, Sullivan. You didn't used to drink."

"I didn't used to do a lot of things, Kay. People change, or didn't you know?"

"Yes, they do. But, still, I—"

"This is the first time I've had more than one or two social drinks in over ten years, so if you're worried I've a drinking problem, kindly forget it."

"I wasn't, Sul—Sullivan, I know you never were a drinker. That's not why I—"

"Then what? Tell me, Kay. What is it? What are you doing here?"

Kay rose and swept around the big room turning on lamps. "I cannot talk to someone I can't see," she told a blinking, frowning Sullivan. She came back to him, shaking her head. "You look a sight, Sullivan."

"I wasn't planning on entertaining." His dark eyes were on the glass he held. Slowly swirling the iceless Scotch, he set the drink on his naked stomach and lifted his eyes to her.

She stood looking down at him. He looked rawly masculine and Kay thought silently he couldn't have been more appealing had he been dressed in a tux.

Again she dropped on the footstool, crossed her arms over her chest and said, "We have to talk, Sullivan. About what happened today in your office."

"What happened today? Did something happen today? If so, I didn't—"

"Don't be flip with me, Sullivan Ward!" Kay's arms came uncrossed and she leaned toward him. "You know very well what I'm talking about. You held me and you—"

Sullivan sighed. "I'm sorry. God, you'd think I'd get tired of saying that, wouldn't you?" He smiled and looked up at her. "I am sorry, Kay. I was out of line and I behaved like a teenager whose hormones were raging."

"That's all it was?"

"What else?"

"I think there's a great deal more to it than hormones, Sullivan. I think that what we had before—"

"Before what?" he growled. "Before you got what you really wanted and left me behind? Before you felt you'd learned all I could teach you? Before you were certain there was no longer any use for me in your little schemes?"

"That's not fair. I never used you, Sullivan, never. You hired me and we..."

With speed and grace that surprised her, Sullivan leaned up and placed both feet on the floor, trapping her inside his bent knees. "Listen to me, Kay, because I'm tired of repeating myself. I gave you your first break because you were talented. Then I fell—then I foolishly began a personal relationship with you because you were so darned sweet and irresistible. It's always foolish to get involved with someone you work with; it's downright destructive when that person is a young, willful girl with burning ambition and the skill and desirability to realize her dreams."

"There was nothing wrong with our relationship, Sullivan. What we had was—"

"Special?" he interrupted icily. "Is that what you're intending to say?" His lips curled cruelly, his eyes snapping.

He tossed down a long swallow of Scotch and leaned back once more.

"It was special, Sullivan. It was. That last night was—"

"A mistake. A terrible blunder on my part, but as I said a while ago, I'm a little sick of saying I'm sorry. Take all the wrongs I've done to you and make a list. Then I'll check it off with the appropriate number of I'm sorry's."

Kay shook her aching head. "I don't want any apologies, I want—I want us to be like we were in your office this afternoon. I want you—"

"To take you to bed?" He slowly leaned forward. "That it, Kay? You have an appetite and want it sated?"

"No, Sullivan, I don't want you to take me to bed," she said sadly, her bottom lip beginning to tremble. "I want you to make love to me. There's a difference, you know."

"Oh, really?" He lifted heavy brows. "Well, thanks, darling, for telling me. I had no idea. I thought sure..."

"Damn you, Sullivan Ward. Don't you patronize me! Do you hear me? What happened between you and me five years ago in the Brown Palace Hotel was an act of love; I know it, you know it. I loved you and you loved me and I'll never believe otherwise."

"So how in hell could you get out of my bed and catch a plane to the coast?" He was back up now, his face close to hers. "Answer that one, little miss authority on human relations!" His eyes were filled with fury. "My God, I couldn't believe it. I made love to you half the night. I told you over and over how much I loved you and I'll be damned if you didn't leave me without so much as a parting kiss. You let me lie there sleeping while you walked right out of my life." A hand went up to rake jerkily through his coal-black hair. "Can you imagine how I felt when I woke to find you gone?" He shook his head as if to clear it.

Tears now streaming down her cheeks, Kay said softly, "Why didn't you tell me to stay? Why? Sul, why didn't you make me stay with you? That's all you would have had to do. I never would have—"

"Stop! Stop it," he said in a voice as cold as the drizzling winter rain streaking down the two-story glass behind them.

"You're a great actress, Kay, but it won't work anymore, at least not with this boy. I've seen the movie, read the book, know all your moves, honey." Sullivan started smiling. "You know, you're like everyone else, me included, you find it almost impossible to face the truth about yourself. Am I right?" Kay looked at him, tears falling freely, unable to stop their flow. "You were ambitious and you got a great offer to go to L.A. Now, you'd have gone anyway if I'd begged you to stay, but since I didn't, it's a great little escape for you, isn't it? You can always piously tell yourself that everything is my fault. Big, bad ol' Sullivan took your virginity. Old loser Sullivan resented your success. Cold, uncaring Sullivan let you go away."

Sullivan shook a cigarette from a pack, lit it and continued speaking. "Well, babe, just between you and me, let's face the facts here. You did exactly what you wanted to do. People usually do, though hardly any of us can ever face it. As for me, well you're right, I resented your success, was jealous of it. That suit you?"

"No, it doesn't," Kay said sadly, wiping her eyes on the back of her hand. "Maybe everything you've said is...is true. Maybe I'm every bit as bad as...."

"I didn't say bad," he interrupted her. "I said you did what you wanted to do."

"Well, maybe that's...Sullivan, I wish I'd never...I want...."

"Too late, darlin'." He waved his smoking cigarette in the air. "Way too late for regrets." He took a long drag. "But cheer up, Kay. Everything works out. You are better than ever on the air. The raw talent you had from the beginning has been skillfully polished."

"Thank you," she said, sniffing.

"So you see, hon, it's just a matter of a few months that you'll be stuck here." Sullivan rose, effortlessly lifted a long leg over her head and walked to the tall glass windows. Looking out at the rain-soaked city, he said, "It's already the middle of October. We go into the Arbitron audience-rating period the first of November. By no later than mid-January, the book will be out. If we get good numbers—and

I'm sure we will—you'll get a New York offer in no time at all." He lifted his bare shoulders and said, "Then that'll be it. You'll be back on your way."

Kay rose, walked to him and lifted a hand to rest on the small of his back. He flinched. "Sullivan," she said softly, savoring the feel of his smooth, warm flesh beneath her fingers, "I'm leaving now, but I'll tell you something, when I get into my bed tonight, I'll be remembering how you held me and kissed me this morning." She paused and sighed. "And you know what, so will you." Kay let her hand fall away. Impulsively she leaned to him, kissed a bare shoulder blade, turned and hurried across the room to her coat.

Sullivan Ward never turned around.

Kay clung to the shiny brass rail in the marble and mirrored elevator, descending to the ground floor so rapidly her quaking stomach seemed to rise to her tight throat. The heavy chrome doors slid open and Kay rushed out into the corridor, running, anxious to get outside.

The helpful doorman who'd let her in minutes earlier looked up, saw her and smiled. She reached him; he put a white-gloved hand to the front door and softly scolded, "You've not forgotten your key, have you?"

"I don't need it," Kay said flatly, pulling the sash of her raincoat tighter. "I won't be coming back."

"Pardon, miss?"

Kay gave the puzzled man a sad smile. "I'm afraid I've lost my lease." She brushed past him and out into the rainy night.

Back at her lonely apartment, Kay shed her wet clothes, took a hot shower and drew on a warm terry robe. She built a fire in the white marble fireplace and, skipping the evening meal, sat on the carpet before the fire, hugging her knees while outside the cold, wet rain continued to fall.

Staring unblinking into the hypnotic flames, Kay kept hearing Sullivan's accusations ringing in her ears. "You did exactly what you wanted to do; people usually do. What you wanted to do...what you wanted to do."

Kay laid a cheek on her knees as again the tears began to fall. What hurt was that Sullivan, as usual, was right. He'd made her finally face the truth, and the truth did hurt. If she'd loved him beyond all else, she'd never have left him. Couldn't have left him. Sullivan knew it all along. Perhaps she had also, but she'd never faced it until now.

Tears of regret dampened the blue terry robe covering Kay's shaking knees. She'd chosen her career over the man she loved and she'd have to live with that choice. Kay lifted her weary head and looked into the fire. Vision blurred by tears, she understood everything clearly for the first time. It had been her fault, not Sullivan's.

Kay lifted the collar of her loose robe and dabbed at her red, puffy eyes. Tiredly she went to her bedroom, turned back the covers, let the robe slip from her shoulders and crawled naked into her bed. She turned out the bedside lamp, casting the room into darkness.

Her bare body craving the man she'd lost, Kay lay in her lonely bed and wondered how Sullivan was spending this rainy Saturday night. In anguish, Kay turned onto her stomach. She winced. The sensitive area of pinkened flesh just above her left breast brushed against the pillow in her jerky move, causing a brief flash of discomfort.

It was nothing compared to the pain in the heart beating just below the abrasion. Kay buried her face in the pillow and murmured aloud, "Sul, oh, Sul, I'm sorry."

Across town, Sullivan Ward switched off the lamp by his bed and slid naked between the sheets. He lay upon his back, hands folded beneath his head, listening to the steady rain pelting against the tall glass windows. Head aching from the Scotch he'd drunk, heart aching from loneliness, Sullivan recalled Kay's words vividly. "When I get into my bed tonight, I'll be remembering how you held me and kissed me this morning...and so will you." Sullivan groaned in the darkness, turned on to his stomach and punched his pillow.

It was a very businesslike Kay Clark who said hello to Sullivan Ward on Monday morning. It was a pleasant, cooperative Sullivan Ward who greeted her, as though the encounter of Saturday had never happened. "We've got ten minutes, Kay." Sullivan looked at his watch. "I forgot to mention to you last week, we've been invited to host a dance the Denver Asthma Society is holding at McNichols Arena. They want us to MC the affair. It's a fifties type sock hop." Sullivan made a face. "They want us to be king and queen of the hop." He lifted wide shoulders. "Can you make it? It's scheduled for this coming Friday night."

"Sure, I can make it." Kay smiled. "Sounds like fun."

"Good." He nodded. "We're supposed to dress the part. You know, wear something like they wore back in the fifties."

"I'll rustle something up," she assured him. Kay started to rise. "It's almost time."

"Yeah." Sullivan nodded. "One more thing, on Halloween night the Thompson Orphans Home is having their annual party for the kids, and I thought, well . . ."

"Count on me," Kay said.

"Kay, it's not a personal appearance." He laughed. "Well, of course, it's a personal appearance. What I mean is, we don't get paid for this one. The dance we're contracted for, but the children's party would strictly be volunteer."

"I'll be there, Sullivan," she assured him. "And I'm happy to do it for free."

"Thanks, Kay. See Janelle about costumes." His face reddened slightly. "You may choose what you'll wear, of course, but the kids are kind of hoping to see a fairy princess." He smiled boyishly and Kay felt her heart thump against her ribs.

"A fairy princess I'll be." she smiled back at him. "Anything else?"

Sullivan got up and came around the desk. Together they headed for the control room to do their morning show. "*Mile High* magazine called last week, they want an interview at our convenience. I said I'd talk to you and give them a call."

"Fine," Kay agreed, "any afternoon this week will suit me."

"I'll set it up," he said, while from the monitor came Dale Kitrell's voice saying, "So stay tuned for the upcoming Sullivan-and-Kay show and I'll be back with you tomorrow..."

"It's for a good cause, it's gonna be a great time, so be there or be square," Sullivan said into his microphone, promoting, as they had all week, the dance at McNichols Arena. He flipped the key, flooding the room with music, stood, stretched his long arms over his head and said to Kay, "So I'll meet you at the arena at seven tonight?"

Kay signed the FCC log, put it aside and looked up at him. "I thought we could—"

"What?" Sullivan's eyes narrowed a little.

"Nothing." She smiled and rose. "I'll meet you there."

"Right. Remember, dress the part."

"Don't worry."

Kay felt like a giggly teenager when she finished dressing that cold Friday night for the dance. She looked at herself one last time in the mirror and wondered if girls actually dressed this way back in the fifties. Several stiff petticoats made her gray-felt circular skirt billow out around her knees. Her white angora sweater was topped with a fuzzy pink collar tied in a bow, pink furry balls dangling from the ends of the ribbon. Her small waist was cinched in with a three-inch-wide leather belt, its color shocking pink. On her feet were black suede penny loafers with coins in the slits. Thick white bobby socks hugged her slender ankles.

Her face, naked of makeup, looked fresh and youthful. Kay ran a brush through her long flowing hair one last time, adjusted the pink hair ribbon and slathered her mouth with an ample amount of fuchsia-pink lipstick. She pressed her lips together and grinned. Kay stepped back, spun around in a circle to test the effect of skirt and petticoats. Satisfied, she left for the big dance.

Sullivan was on a makeshift stage at the north end of the arena everyone in Denver referred to as "Big Mac." A huge blue-satin banner with "Q102" emblazoned in gold draped the platform. Sound men and engineers were working with a tangle of cables for the sound system. The huge hard-wood floor, used for basketball in the winter, was already filling with people, all dressed in various ensembles of an era past. Overhead, crepe-paper streamers and hundreds of balloons fell from the high ceiling, giving the massive structure the appearance of a school gym decorated for a prom.

Sullivan, intently flipping through a pile of records stacked on a long table near the microphones, didn't notice Kay climbing the stairs to the stage. Kay was given the opportunity to carefully study him while he remained caught up in his task.

Her heart, under the fuzzy white sweater, skipped a beat at the sight of him. Sullivan wore charcoal-gray trousers, pegged in at the ankles. His long-sleeved shirt was of bright pink, his jacket of black leather. His coal-black hair had been greased down into the semblance of a ducktail, though it was already rebelling, springing back to its natural full-ness.

Sullivan finished separating the records into several groups. He shrugged out of his black leather jacket, toss-ing it to a chair. Kay watched, fascinated. Unbuttoning his cuffs, he rolled up pink shirt-sleeves over his forearms, glanced at his watch and stuffed his hands into the pockets of his gray wool slacks.

Dressed as a fifties heartthrob, he looked different, but as appealing as ever. Watching him, Kay decided Sullivan would look good no matter what he wore. Or didn't wear. He was all male. Clothed or naked, his lean body held an animal grace and beauty that couldn't be hidden.

Sullivan looked up.

His face broke into a grin and he started toward her. Feeling suddenly shy and ill-at-ease, as if she were a teen-ager at a dance, Kay tugged nervously at the hem of her white sweater and mouthed the word, "Hi."

He reached her, took her elbow and looking down at her said honestly, "You look so young and cute, Kay. I'd swear you were no more than sixteen or seventeen."

Blushing, she looked up at him and smiled. "You're very much a cool cat yourself tonight, Sullivan."

Sullivan laughed, curled his lip up, ala Elvis, and drew her up to the microphone set up in the middle of the stage. "The mike's not on yet, Kay, so before I turn it on, I thought we'd go over what we're expected to do here this evening." He released her arm and took a seat on the edge of the long table.

Kay stood facing him, hands clutched in front of her. "I guess it'll just be like doing our show from here, right?"

Sullivan lit a cigarette and smiled. "Yeah, that's about it. But they may expect us to...to dance with each other a couple of times, and, too, they are going to crown us king and queen of the hop." Sullivan rolled his eyes upward.

Kay shook her head. "That won't be so bad, will it?"

"No—" he dropped his eyes "—but—"

"But what?"

Sullivan looked up. "Hell, we're supposed...they want us..." Sullivan's words trailed away and his eyes went to Kay's mouth. "Never mind," he said, rising to turn on their mikes.

The dance was soon in full swing as couples of all ages filled the hall and laughingly spun around on the polished floor. Sullivan and Kay played the hit records of an earlier decade and stood before their microphones moving their bodies in time to the tunes, and flirted and teased each other to the delight of the crowd.

Sullivan grabbed his microphone. "This next record has got to be one of the all-time oldies but goodies. Remember 'Jailhouse Rock' by the King? Sure you do! Come on, you people sitting way up there in the cheap seats. Let's rock this joint. I want to see everyone down on the floor. Kay, baby," he continued, speaking into the mike, "wanna show 'em how it's done?"

"Why, Sullivan," she said into her mike, "I'd love to dance with you."

"Well, all right, everybody, let's dance!" Sullivan shouted. He hurriedly cued the record and grabbed Kay's hand. He stepped off the high stage, put his hands to her small waist and lifted her down.

Sullivan took Kay in his arms. She laughed and followed his easy lead. He spun her around and watched appreciatively as her full skirt and petticoats swirled out, rising high on long, shapely legs. Lost in the lively spirit of the dance, they whirled in rhythm to the fast-paced Elvis record and Kay tossed her head in abandon, letting the long, silvery hair sway around her face and shoulders until it was a tumbled mass in her face.

It was Sullivan, his eyes flashing, who reached out to push the silvery mane from her eyes just as the record ended and Kay collapsed against him, breathless, face flushed, heart pounding.

"You okay?" Sullivan's lips were in her hair.

Managing only to nod her head, Kay clung to him, her face pressed to the smooth pink cotton covering his chest. Beneath her ear, his heavy heartbeat speeded. Sullivan's hands came to her shoulders and he gently set her away from him. Kay looked up at him, licking her dry lips. A muscle in his brown jaw flexed furiously. "Back to work," he said, leading her to the stage.

Over an hour later, Sullivan said, almost apologetically to Kay, "We really should dance again." His hand was covering the open mike.

"I can stand it if you can," she quipped, her blue eyes challenging him.

Ignoring the remark, he moved his hand, leaned to the microphone and said in a deep, resonant voice, "I'm going to change the pace. This next song is slow and romantic, so grab that girl you've been dreaming about, this record may do the trick."

By the time the sweet, soft sound of Rosemary Clooney singing the old favorite "Hey There" drifted through the big gym, Sullivan had again lifted Kay from the stage. She was smiling when he slowly pulled her into his embrace. Taking her hand in his, he draped an arm loosely around her waist. Kay ran her other hand slowly over his shirtfront before lifting it up around his neck. Fingertips rested on his nape as the lights dimmed and the laughter and talking quieted and couples throughout the big hall danced dreamily cheek to cheek.

Sullivan and Kay did not dance cheek to cheek. Sullivan looked down into Kay's eyes, though neither spoke. Their gazes locked, Kay finally felt the gentle pressure of Sullivan's hand at her waist, urging her closer. Sighing, she closed the small gap between them as Sullivan dropped her hand and put both arms around her. Kay pressed her face into the warmth of his throat while her hand spread on the wall of his chest. Her lips were almost touching him and she longed to press her mouth to that smooth skin, to open her lips and taste him, to lick away tiny beads of perspiration.

They moved as one body, graceful, effortlessly gliding around the floor, eyes closed, enjoying the wonder of being in each other's arms. Kay became vitally aware of the strong, throbbing pulse in Sullivan's throat. Its steady beat so near her parted lips brought a shiver of excitement that was felt by Sullivan. Instinctively, he pressed her closer and Kay felt her sweatered breasts flattening against his hard chest. His knee went between her legs and Kay guiltily wished she weren't wearing so many clothes; the full frilly petticoats made contact vague and fleeting.

Wistfully wanting this slow, romantic song to go on forever, Kay let her spread hand glide upward to the open V of Sullivan's shirt. She itched to touch that crisp hair so tantalizingly curling there. Just as the tips of her fingers made contact, the record ended, the lights came up and Kay and Sullivan separated.

"Thank you," Sullivan said shakily, and Kay, blinking up at him, nodded vigorously.

When the hour neared midnight, the president of the Asthma Society stepped onto the stage, took over the mike and made a short speech. After thanking everyone for coming and assuring them that the proceeds from the successful affair would be put to good use, he announced that it was time to crown the king and queen.

Helpers appeared and to Kay's delighted embarrassment, she was crowned queen. A rhinestone tiara was pinned atop her hair and a short red-velvet cape was draped around her shoulders. She was handed a dozen red roses and the tall, lanky president stooped and gave her a peck on the cheek.

Then it was Sullivan's turn. A curvaceous brunette placed a gold-painted crown on his head and draped a purple cape around his broad shoulders. Hooking the white fur collar under his chin, the girl smiled coyly and said, "I've always wanted the chance to kiss you, Sullivan."

She looped her arms around his neck, pulled his head down and gave his mouth a kiss. The crowd cheered as she released him and Sullivan made a short speech of thanks. Kay stood stiffly listening while the girl who had kissed Sullivan stood beside him. Jealousy causing her stomach to ache painfully, Kay found it very hard to continue smiling.

The president was again speaking and Kay heard only the last few words. "...the best king and queen we've ever had." Loud applause from the audience. "And a handsome couple if ever there was one. I think the king should kiss his queen."

Kay stood statue still, the roses in her arms. She could feel color rising to her face. She cast a wary glance at Sullivan and saw to her surprise that he was smiling easily. Self-assured and gallant, he nodded to the eager faces looking up at them, turned to Kay and brought a hand up her waist, drawing her into the curve of his arm.

Taking the big bouquet of roses from her ice-cold hands, he laid them aside, smiled and whispered against her temple, "This is the part I forgot to warn you about. Relax, I won't really kiss you."

He gently turned her to him. A thumb came up to her chin, tilted her face upward and he bent to her. His warm mouth tenderly touched hers, male lips shut, cautiously, carefully fitting themselves to the soft, curving mouth under his. His mouth didn't stay closed for long. The sweet, honeyed lips beneath his were slightly parted. Sullivan's mouth opened instinctively and he gently nipped at her bottom lip. Kay's mouth opened wide in response. Sullivan shuddered. Mindless of the crowd staring up at them, he pulled her closer, fitting her small body to his. Kay sighed and clung to him while a long arm tightened around her and a brown hand came up to cup a delicate cheek. Sullivan, dark eyes closed, breathed into her mouth; Kay swayed and sucked in the hot breath, making it her own.

Sullivan lifted his head. He stood holding her for a moment, looking down into her eyes. Reality crept in and he dropped his hands from her, smiled down at the fans and said, "First time I've ever kissed a queen."

Six

––––––

On Halloween, the first snow swirled down from the high country, blanketing the city of Denver. Unable to sleep, Kay rose and dressed warmly, deciding she'd go to the station early and tape some of the records that were beginning to wear.

Casting a look at Cheeseman Park far below, Kay smiled. It was rapidly becoming a glistening winter wonderland, a sight she'd missed terribly when she'd worked on the west coast. Kay drew on a down jacket and left, maneuvering her little red car down the deserted snow-covered streets.

At ten minutes past five, she arrived at the station. Pulling off her jacket, Kay tossed it over the back of her chair, stripped off her leather gloves and stepped out of her tall fur-lined boots. Off came the white wool cap, and Kay shook out her hair. She pulled down on her bulky green sweater and began the search for the blank cartridges.

Kay remembered Janelle moving the new tapes into Sullivan's office, explaining there was more room for them there than in the control room or the production studio.

Kay hurried down the dim hallway toward Sullivan's office. Stepping inside, she closed the door and went directly to his big desk, flipping on the gooseneck lamp on its top. She went around the desk, jerked out the bottom drawer and reached in to pick up several blank cartridges. Straightening, she saw him.

Kay closed the drawer without taking anything from it. She was no longer concerned with the tapes because across the room, stretched out on the long leather couch, was Sullivan Ward. White shirt open down his chest, he was sleeping soundly. One long arm was bent beneath his head, the other was folded over his waist. His loafers were on the floor beside the sofa; his feet were crossed at the ankles.

His face looked innocent and peaceful in repose, despite the stubble of a black beard covering his jaws. His eyes were closed, long, sweeping lashes resting on high, pronounced cheekbones. Sensual, wide lips were slightly parted over even white teeth. His hair was disheveled and falling over his forehead.

Sullivan moaned softly in his sleep and turned his head a little. Kay, her heart hammering against her ribs, tiptoed around the desk, drawn helplessly to his sleeping form. How she longed to go to him, to reach out and smooth back an errant lock of hair. How she wanted to trace the fullness of those male lips with a tingling finger. How she ached to have those long dark eyelashes flutter against her face. How she craved to press a cheek to that warm, furred chest.

The dark, liquid eyes opened. Kay, standing just above him, made no effort to move away. It was too late for that. His eyes, though still glazed with sleep, held a warm inviting look. Slowly he raised a hand from his stomach and held it out to her. Kay, trembling slightly, took the offered hand and, looking only into his eyes, felt herself being gently pulled down onto the long sofa.

She said nothing, nor did Sullivan. She knew only that she was now on the couch with him, her body pressed to its tall back. Sullivan was facing her, lying on his side. As though it were a completely natural, an everyday occurrence, he

pressed his long, sleep-warm body to hers and with eyes
closing once more, his mouth met hers.

It was a slow, warm, unhurried kiss, as though he had all
the rest of the day to do nothing else but this. Kay, her body
warmed by the heated, rock-hard frame pressed against her,
let those warm, persuasive lips do what they would. Sullivan's mouth moved languidly upon hers, tasting, enjoying,
sleepily exploring and savoring. Not daring to break the
spell, Kay, afraid even to lift her arms around him, waited
for him to leisurely part her lips with his tongue.

He did and Kay bit back her sigh of pleasure. Sullivan's
tongue swept the dark recesses of her mouth, stroking her
with deliberate, lazy, heart-stopping tenderness that was
more erotic than any forceful, demanding kiss could possibly have been. Thinking fleetingly that he intended to kiss
her forever, so long was the caress, and thinking what a
lovely way to spend the cold, snowy dawn, Kay unconsciously sighed into Sullivan's mouth.

His lips never leaving hers, Sullivan shifted slightly. Kay
found she was now on her back, Sullivan above her, his
torso pressing down on hers, a jean-clad knee nudging between her own. And still he kissed her.

Kay cautiously slid her hands inside his open shirt, glo-
rying in the feel of the warm, bare skin of his smooth back.
It was Sullivan's turn to sigh into her mouth and a hand
went to the hem of Kay's bulky green sweater. He pushed
the scratchy wool up a few inches, stopping short of her
breasts. Then his bare torso was back on hers and the three
or four inches of Kay's bare midriff touching his naked flesh
made him shudder. His lips left hers and he buried his face
in her long tousled hair and inhaled deeply of her sweet fragrance while Kay clung to him and whispered his name.

His heartbeat thudding, Sullivan seemed to be fighting
desperately for control, a battle Kay hoped he would lose.
After what seemed an eternity of indecision, Sullivan slowly
lifted his head and looked down at her. His expressive eyes
told her it was she who'd lost, not he.

"I could blame it on being half asleep," he said tiredly,
lithely levering himself from her, "but I won't." He stood

above her, raking a hand through his hair, his eyes very pointedly avoiding the bare female ribs he'd exposed. Buttoning his shirt, he turned from her.

Kay, slowly sitting up, tugged the sweater back down over her hips and said softly, "Do you have to blame it on anything? Can't we just admit that it's what we both want?"

"No," he turned back to face her. "What are you doing here at this hour?" He glanced at his gold watch.

Kay picked up his loafers from beside the sofa. "Doesn't matter. What about you, you fill in for one of the jocks?"

Sullivan nodded. "Dale's wife went into labor. Can I have my shoes?" He held out a hand.

Kay smiled. "Have you heard yet? Has she delivered?"

"A boy. Came around three this morning; they're both fine. Dale called, elated."

"That's wonderful." Kay motioned him to his chair.

In no mood to argue, Sullivan slid into the swivel chair. "Ace was up listening to the radio, heard me in Dale's time slot and came in around four-thirty to take over. He's a good kid. Kay, give me my shoes."

"Ace is a sweet boy," she said, circling the desk, his shoes in her hands. "You must be dead; you couldn't have slept more than fifteen minutes before I interrupted you."

Sullivan shook a cigarette from a pack, lit it and said, "I'm fine, I—what the hell are you doing?"

Kay, ignoring the unpleasantness in his voice, knelt before his chair. "Lift your right foot," she commanded and, dumbfounded, he obeyed. Kay slipped his shoe on, biting her lip as she worked to get the stubborn heel to slide into place. That accomplished, she turned to his left foot.

Head bent, Kay sat on her heels between his legs, tugging at the shoe. Above her, Sullivan sat looking down at the shiny silver head bent to her task. "This is hardly necessary." He did his best to sound disgusted.

"I know." She tossed her hair back and smiled up at him. "I don't want you to catch cold."

With his help, Kay managed to get both shoes on his feet and Sullivan let out a sigh of relief. Now she'd rise and put some distance between them so he could breathe again. But

to his shocked surprise, Kay remained seated on her heels
between his legs. Every muscle in his long right leg con-
stricted when she impulsively leaned toward him and laid her
head upon his bent knee. Sullivan watched in stunned fas-
cination while she brushed her soft cheek against his taut
thigh and said softly, "Sullivan, dear Sullivan, can't we
please start over?"

Sullivan crushed out his half-smoked cigarette, sighed and
brought a hand to the silvery crown of her head. Kay smiled
and closed her eyes. Gently he stroked her hair and said in
a choked soft voice, "No. No, Kay, we can't."

Kay slowly lifted her head. "But why?"

His hand left her hair. He pushed back his chair and rose.
He stood towering over her. Kay, her head thrown back, was
looking up at him. "Because, Kay," he said truthfully, his
hard jaw flexing, "I'm afraid of you, as I've never been of
anyone else in my life."

It continued to snow throughout the cold, gray day. The
annual Halloween party for the Thompson Orphans Home
was scheduled for seven o'clock at the Marriott, and all the
air personalities were to attend. Kay, dressed as a fairy
princess, deposited her heavy camel coat with a smiling
bellman and crossed the lushly carpeted lobby, passing a
huge rock fireplace, snapping and crackling, its flames
shooting high up its tall chimney.

Groups of upholstered couches near the fire's warmth
were occupied by people drinking mugs of Irish coffee while
they talked. Kay drew their attention and felt momentarily
foolish sweeping past them in a strapless white satin gown
with a magic wand in her hand. Their laughter made her
ears turn red. She quickened her pace, eager to get down the
dark-paneled corridor to the last door on the right. Behind
it was the banquet room where tonight's party would be
held.

Kay stepped into the room and her eyes immediately
found Sullivan. Freshly showered and shaved, he looked
virilely handsome in a pair of snug-fitting beige wool slacks.
A soft cashmere sweater of the same hue draped perfectly

across wide shoulders and chest. His dark eyes were sparkling and he looked not the least bit tired though he'd not slept, save for the half hour on his office couch.

Kay started toward him. He looked up, saw her and that odd, half glad, half sad expression flitted across his features. It was gone instantly and he smiled warmly and nodded. Kay, again feeling very foolish in the white satin evening gown with its tight waist and bodice, its full gathered skirt covered with an overskirt of silver and white-striped taffeta, smiled nervously. A silver crown was pinned securely on her head and her hair was brushed out, cascading around her bare shoulders and down her back. In her right hand she carried a magic wand. Wishing she could touch it to the wide shoulder of the handsome, dark-haired man looking at her, instantly making him hers, Kay swallowed and went to meet him.

"You look lovely," he said in a calm, deep voice. "The kids will love you. You look like a real fairy princess." Without thinking, he lifted a hand to push a charmingly rebellious lock of hair from her cheek. His eyes dropped to the swell of her breasts above the tight, shimmering bodice. Immediately they flicked back up to her face as he shoved his hands into the pockets of his wool pants and said, "They'll be here any minute now."

From the double doors at the far side of the room, an explosion of noise made further conversation not only unnecessary, but impossible. Over two hundred kids, aged three to twelve years, poured into the hall, shouting and laughing. Five harried guardians were with the boisterous group, herding the youngsters to the white-clothed tables. The room was suddenly alive with the zest of happy youth and when Kay looked up at Sullivan's hard, handsome face, she saw that he wore an easy smile of affection for the yelling, squirming roomful of children.

"Excuse me, Kay," he said politely and disappeared into the crowd, ruffling the hair of a child's head here, shaking the hand of a grinning youngster there.

The meal was served and two hundred young people ate as though they had never eaten before. After a main course that included roast beef, broiled trout or fried chicken served with mounds of creamed potatoes, green beans, sweet corn, buttered carrots and hot rolls, oohs and aahs escaped young lips as a huge jack-o'-lantern-shaped cake was rolled in. Under sticky orange icing, rich chocolate cake was moist and mouth-wateringly delicious. Ice cream was served with the cake and there was also pumpkin pie, pecan pie and chocolate-chip cookies.

When the hungriest of the boys had had their fill of cake and ice cream, Sullivan rose and clapped his hands for silence. He made a short speech to the full, happy group and drew loud applause when he told them in closing that there was a gift awaiting each of them. The words were hardly out of his mouth before he signaled Jeff, Ace Black and brand-new papa Dale Kitrell to pass out the gaily wrapped packages. Squeals arose as tiny hands tore into big boxes to find warm, colorful down-filled jackets inside.

Sullivan, watching with pleasure, looked up at Kay and inclined his dark head, inviting her to join him at the podium. Kay made her way across the room to him. Smiling easily, he put a long arm lightly around her small waist, lowered his lips to her ear and whispered, "Kay, if you will, they'd love to hear you say a few words, all right?"

Throat tight, she nodded and wondered if her vocal cords would work with him standing so close. She looked up at him and he must have read her thoughts.

"Forget it, Kay, you've done your part. I've seen the lovable little rascals tugging at you all evening. There's been so many tiny hands on that dress, I'm surprised it's remained white." He grinned engagingly and released her waist.

Relaxing a little, she smiled and agreed. "I know. I've been pulled at all night, but I haven't minded, really. They think I truly am a fairy princess, I suppose."

"Aren't you?" Sullivan teased and Kay felt her pulse grow erratic. Before she could respond, he left her side. The party continued and more little hands, some with traces of chocolate cake on them, grasped at Kay's shiny dress. She talked to the children, held them on her lap, hugged them and enjoyed every minute.

By the time the guardians were lining up the children to load them back onto the waiting buses, Kay was exhausted. Rubbing her neck, she dropped into a deserted chair and jumped when Jeff touched her bare shoulder, jerked a chair around near hers and straddled it.

"Will you look at that?" he said, directing her attention to the far side of the room, near the entrance. Sullivan sat in an overstuffed chair against the wall. On his lap, a child of three or four was held in his long arms. The child, as fair as Sullivan was dark, was sound asleep, his golden head resting on Sullivan's broad chest. Sullivan's arm supported the boy's back and his dark cheek was atop the child's head. Sullivan, too, was sound asleep. The pair slept peacefully, unaware of the loud commotion going on all around them.

The maternal instinct in every female surfaced grippingly as Kay stared, transfixed, at the two. Sullivan looked as much the innocent little boy as the child in his arms. That he loved children had been in undisguised evidence all night. He handled them with an understanding and tenderness that was beautiful to witness. Her chest aching with love for him, Kay, completely forgetting Jeff seated beside her, trembled a little, thinking how fulfilling it would be to have Sullivan Ward's babies.

"You really ought to give him one of those some day." Jeff drew her attention back to him.

"What?" Kay blinked at him.

Jeff grinned. "You know what I said, C.A."

"Jeff, it's too late," Kay said sadly.

"Is it?" He grinned, his eyes sparkling. He rose. "In that case, I've got three little monsters at home I'll loan out to anyone that'll take 'em. Night, hon."

Jeff walked away and Kay's eyes drifted back to the sleeping pair across the room. Knowing her deepest, most private feelings must be written all over her face, Kay shoved back the chair and hurriedly fled the room. Retrieving her coat, she turned up the collar around her cold throat and rushed out into the snowy night alone.

* * *

The November issue of *Mile High* magazine hit the newsstands on the first day of the month, the very day the Arbitron rating period began at Q102 and at every other radio station in town. On the magazine's slick cover, a handsome couple smiled into the camera.

A fair young woman with deep blue eyes and with silver hair feathered around her small, oval face stood directly in front of a strikingly handsome man. Since he was much taller than the woman, the man's strong chin rested lightly atop her head, ruffling her hair. A long sweatered arm was wrapped around the woman's shoulders in front, reaching completely across her. The woman's hands were raised, holding that muscular arm.

Both wore warm, happy smiles.

Beneath the photo, the caption read, "Denver's hottest duo." Inside, a well-written story about the pair spread over six pages with more photographs of Sullivan and Kay.

Arbitron audience ratings soon got underway, and Sullivan and Kay outdid themselves to make their morning show entertaining. To further insure success, they increased their personal appearances, sometimes doing as many as three a week. It was great for the show; everywhere they appeared, be it the opening of a new nightclub, an expensive ski shop or a pro basketball game. They were mobbed by eager fans, many carrying a copy of *Mile High* magazine, which they thrust anxiously at the good-looking couple for autographs.

Sam Shults was fully approving, urging the pair to get out and be seen at every opportunity. Kay was more than eager to make the needed appearances. Not only was it beneficial for the station, it constantly threw her and Sullivan together. She kept hoping that in time, if she were very, very patient, he'd come around. She had decided that she'd never again push him or plead with him. He was a proud and stubborn man and she knew her Sul well enough to realize that he, and he alone, would be the aggressor should he change his mind. There was little she could do but try to show him, by her actions, that she could be trusted. She could prove that she wanted no other man, that she would not try to press or bully him.

She could do nothing but wait.

As though he could sense the unspoken change in Kay, Sullivan seemed to relax. There were no more kisses, no tortured glances, no evidence of strain and stress written on his features. Kay wasn't sure if that was good or bad, but she reasoned that if they were to ever recover the closeness that had once been theirs, they'd first need to become friends. That's how it had happened all those years before. They'd been good friends, going to lunch together, talking for hours, selecting new music, discussing everything under the sun. Until that cold morning she'd rushed into the control room and Sullivan had smiled, risen and kissed her for the first time.

Thanksgiving came and Kay, Sullivan, Jeff and the rest of the crew took part in what was referred to as "Cowboy Bill's Annual Thanksgiving Dinner." A big, burly man with a heart as large as his person, Cowboy Bill had organized and given his time and money to this worthwhile project for over twenty years.

Grateful, hungry people showed up by mid-morning outside a spacious leased warehouse. There, dozens of turkeys were being sliced, tubs of dressing being stirred, and the aroma of freshly baked pumpkin pies permeated the air.

Kay, Sullivan and the Q102 crew, white dish towels tied around their waists, acted as waiters. They were joined by other area radio and television personalities and by the time the last slice of white meat had been enjoyed, hundreds of diners had been served.

It was a lovely day for Kay. Sullivan, in a jovial mood, hurried between the long tables with platters of food on his arm. More than once, he'd caught her eye across the room, and smiled as if to say isn't this fun? Isn't this like old times?

After the big meal had been served and the crowd had departed, the working media teams sat down to eat. Sullivan, a plate piled high with turkey, dressing and all the trimmings, was the last to come to the table. Kay, already seated, felt her heart speed just a bit when he came to stand directly behind her and said teasingly, "Is this seat taken?"

"Damn straight it is," said the devilish Jeff Kerns, scooting closer to Kay. He shot a look up at Sullivan, daring him.

Sullivan, carefully balancing his full plate in one big hand, bent close to Jeff's ear. "Move over, Kerns, you're in my spot."

Kay said nothing, but she smiled warmly at the man who gracefully slid over the bench and took his place beside her, gently nudging Jeff aside. "You don't mind, do you?" Sullivan's eyes were on her face. Those expressive eyes held a warm, shining light.

Kay smiled at him and made no reply. None was necessary. He knew very well she didn't mind.

It was nighttime when they all exited the warehouse. Kay remained silent when Sullivan possessively took her arm and guided her to her waiting Porsche. Calling their good nights to the others, they walked across the crunchy ground. Sullivan, the collar of his tan cashmere coat turned up around his cold ears, smiled down at Kay, and she gave fleeting consideration to inviting him over for coffee or a drink.

"Kay," Sullivan said as they reached her car, "you drive carefully."

She turned to face him. "Sullivan, I—"

"Yes?" he was looking down at her, standing very close, his dark hair blowing in the cold winter wind.

"Happy Thanksgiving."

"It was, wasn't it," he said, turned and went to his Mercedes.

Rating period ended on December fifteenth, and at ten o'clock on that date, Sullivan Ward turned off his mike, rose from his chair and let out a loud shout of relief. Kay, laughing, stood up, stuck out her hand and said merrily, "Shake, partner. We did it!"

"We sure did, baby," Sullivan said, and ignoring her outstretched hand, wrapped his long arms around her and crushed her to his tall frame. He rocked her back and forth

in uninhibited glee and Kay thought she would surely die of
happiness. Instinctively, she molded her small body to his,
loving the warmth and strength of that very male physique
pressing against her. Tentatively lifting her hands, she put
them to Sullivan's trim waist. The rocking ceased. The
laughter died. Sullivan, as though coming fully to his senses,
eased her away from him.

"Okay, you guys—" Jeff stuck his head in the door
"—it's time to celebrate. Be at Leo's in fifteen minutes for
champagne brunch." He was gone before they replied.

"Hungry?" Sullivan smiled down at her.

"Famished," she replied.

"Shall we?" He took her hand in his.

"You bet." She clung to his hand and they both laughed
and giggled like children when, in their elation, they completely forgot to don their coats and almost froze crossing
Broadway in the frigid December air.

Betty Shults, Sam's happy wife, insisted on having the
station Christmas party at their impressive home in the
foothills of West Denver. Begging Kay to come over early
and help out, Betty really wanted the opportunity to visit
with Kay before the other guests arrived. Kay agreed, and
shortly before six o'clock on the appointed date, she arrived at the Shults home dressed in a long, lush, figure-
hugging dress of jet-black velvet.

She'd bought the dress for the occasion and she didn't try
to fool herself: she picked it with Sullivan in mind. She
wanted to draw his attention. To make him notice her. To
appear sophisticated and alluring.

"My stars." Betty clasped her plump hands together and
stared at Kay. "You are breathtaking; how can he possibly
go on resisting you?" She took Kay's coat.

"Who?" Kay asked innocently.

Betty hugged her velvet-clad slender arm and drew Kay
toward the big, cheerful den. "Don't be coy. Sullivan Ward.
That's who!"

Kay sighed wearily. "Betty, does the entire world go
around speculating on the relationship of Sullivan and me?"

"Why, no, dear, only those of us who love you both. I know I shouldn't tell tales out of school, but . . . well, Kay, when you left here before, Sullivan was like a wounded animal. I mean he was—"

"Please, Betty," Kay entreated. "That was a long time ago. I assure you that Sullivan Ward is completely whole again."

"Is he now?" Betty put her hands to her hips and tilted her head to one side.

"Is who what?" Sam Shults came into the room pulling on his suit jacket.

Betty furiously gave Kay eye signals indicating that to reveal what she'd just said would put her in hot water with her husband. Kay, more than relieved to let the subject be dropped and forgotten, said diplomatically, "I was just telling Betty that Sullivan is almost sure we're going to be getting the best rating book ever."

"No question about it." Sam Shults shook his head decisively. "And I lay the success all at your pretty little feet, Kay."

Soon the doorbell chimes were ringing out the first eleven notes of "Jingle Bells" as guests began arriving. With each chiming of the bell, Kay, a glass of eggnog in her hand, looked anxiously toward the doorway, awaiting Sullivan's entrance.

Jeff Kerns and his attractive wife came in with the Kitrells. Sherry Jones, her auburn hair dressed dramatically atop her head, was proudly clinging to the muscular arm of Ace Black, and it was evident by the pleased look in her big green eyes that she was more than thrilled that the shy, boyishly handsome disc jockey had finally fallen under the spell she'd been vigorously weaving around him.

Laughter and loud talk soon filled the room as guests arrived in an unending stream. The chief engineer, the salespeople with their spouses and dates, the news team. Almost everyone from the station was there. Yet for Kay, no one was there because Sullivan Ward had not yet arrived.

Switching from eggnog to pink champagne, Kay laughed and talked and kept a nervous watch on the door. Finally she heard the warm, deep voice like no other on earth and she drew a sharp breath, took a big swallow of champagne and casually turned around.

He stood across the room, towering above the crowd. His thick black hair was carefully groomed, his dark jaws freshly shaven and shiny clean. He was smiling easily, his teeth starkly white in his swarthy, handsome face. He wore a well-tailored jacket of black velvet, his snowy white shirt set off with a black silk tie. He was breathtakingly handsome. He was ruggedly male. He was cocksure without being arrogant. He was all a woman could want.

On his arm was Janelle Davis.

Sullivan, his arm bent for Janelle's hand to rest inside, unbuttoned his black jacket, pushed it back and slid his other hand into the pocket of his gray wool slacks. He looked across the room. Then he saw her.

His dark gaze came to rest on Kay. She, and she alone, saw his eyes widen minutely. Kay, clinging to the crystal champagne glass for dear life, inhaled, unconsciously swelling her breasts to strain against the snug black velvet.

Sullivan's hand clenched inside his pants pocket. She was across the room looking directly at him and never in all the years he'd known her had she looked more desirable than she did on this cold December night. She leaned casually against the cocktail bar, which stretched the length of the den's far wall. Her dress was of velvet as black as the jacket he wore. Long tight sleeves covered her slim arms, reaching almost to her delicate knuckles. Fleetingly, Sullivan thought the sleeves were the only modest part of the gorgeous dress. Supple velvet barely covered creamy white shoulders. A daring neckline plunged well below the valley of her full, lush breasts and it was there his heated gaze was drawn. Rounded mounds of alabaster curved seductively. Should she move too suddenly, Sullivan was certain she'd cause a scandal.

Tearing his eyes away from the promise of what lay just inside that tight bodice, he leisurely assessed what remained. The skirt, long and tight, was slit up past her knees on both sides. He got a glimpse of a long, stockinged leg, bent at the knee, a small foot in a black satin pump. He jerked his eyes back to her face. She was not smiling, but she was still looking directly at him.

She'd worn her hair swept up off her neck. It was arranged in a too-professional-looking array of curls interlaced with little black velvet bows. The dancing blue eyes were on him, the delicious lips were slightly parted.

Sullivan wanted to choke her.

Sullivan wanted to make love to her.

"She does look lovely, doesn't she?" Janelle's voice held a sad note of resignation.

Sullivan tore his eyes from the vision in black velvet to look down at the attractive face turned up to his. "Who?" he said, color suffusing his face beneath the darkness of his smooth skin.

Janelle squeezed his arm. "Get me a drink will you, Sullivan?" Lowering her voice to a mere whisper, she added, "and you needn't rush to get back with it."

Sullivan patted the small hand resting in the crook of his arm. "I'll be back in five minutes flat. Champagne? Eggnog?"

"Make it Scotch." Janelle smiled sweetly, released his arm and turned to talk with Jeff Kerns's wife.

Sullivan made his way leisurely to the bar, greeting friends as he went. Kay watched him approach, took another healthy sip of champagne and pretended a calm she didn't feel. Then he was standing beside her. To Sam Shults, tending bar, he said, "Sammy, a Scotch mist for Janelle and I'll have—" his head turned and he was looking down at Kay "—a coronary from that dress." He smiled lazily and Kay never noticed his hands clutching the polished wood of the bar.

"Does that mean you approve or disapprove?" Kay could feel heat rising to her throat as his eyes brazenly went to her breasts and stayed.

"Here's the Scotch for Janelle." Sam Shults set the glass on the bar. "Now, Sullivan, what was it you said you want?"

Sullivan's eyes reluctantly came back to Sam. "I don't think what I want would be good for me, so I'll pass for now." He cut his eyes at Kay and her heart plummeted. His message had been clear. She lifted her small chin, leaned close to his ear and said, "It would be very good for you, so don't pass forever."

Before he could respond, she turned and walked regally away, and she could feel his eyes follow her as she went.

Kay wanted to choke him.

Kay wanted to make love to him.

Two days prior to Christmas, Kay flew to Phoenix, Arizona, to meet her parents at her uncle's home in Scottsdale. Before she left, she knocked lightly on Sullivan's closed door and went inside. In her hand she carried a slim box wrapped in silver paper.

Sullivan looked up, rose and said, "So you're off to the airport?"

"My plane leaves in an hour," she confirmed. "I just wanted to give you your present before I go."

"Kay," he said, grimacing, "you shouldn't have. I didn't want you to—"

She thrust the package at him. "I wanted to. It's not much, please open it."

Sullivan took the box and patiently worked the ribbon and paper away. "Just what I needed." He smiled warmly at her, looking at the gold pen inside. He lifted it out and turned it in his thumb and forefinger.

"No, Sullivan," Kay said softly, "there's no inscription." He looked at her, knowing she was referring to the inscribed gold lighter she'd given him that other Christmas. "I must run, I'll—"

"Wait, Kay." He laid the pen aside, pulled out the middle drawer of his desk and lifted out a small box. Shyly he handed it to her.

Kay looked at him, dumbfounded. She clutched the box and stared at him. "Thank you," she finally managed and started backing away.

"It's nothing, Kay, but why don't you open it."

"Sure," she said, and tore eagerly into the package. Inside, she found a soft red-leather case, and inside the case was a tiny camera no larger than a cigarette lighter. It was of shiny yellow gold.

"It actually works," Sullivan announced, watching her study the delicate little camera. "And you'll be needing it."

Kay's eyes lifted to his. "Thank you."

"You're supposed to ask me why you'll need it." Sullivan was circling his desk toward her.

Gently rubbing the camera's shiny surface, Kay lifted her wide blue eyes. "Why?"

Sullivan grinned. "Because you and I are escorting a planeload of people to Paradise Island in the Bahamas in mid-January." He loved the surprised expression on her face.

"Sullivan, you mean it?"

"I'll tell you all about it when you get back." He took her arm and guided her toward the door. "Have a merry Christmas, Kay."

"You, too, Sullivan," she said, and felt his warm lips brush her cheek. Her face lit up like a Christmas tree. "Oh, you, too!"

It was warm and lovely in Phoenix. Kay was happy to see her parents, who'd flown up from Florida. Uncle Will had decorated his palatial hillside home with every kind of ornament and Aunt Sybil had obviously been cooking for weeks.

Kay received loads of lovely gifts from her well-heeled family. So all were puzzled when, the very day after Christmas, Kay rose early, ate a large breakfast and announced she was going to spend the day shopping.

Ignoring the questioning eyes turned on her, Kay gave her mother and dad a quick kiss. She borrowed one of her uncle's cars and headed for the exclusive Scottsdale shops with a mysterious smile on her face.

There was one thing on her mind. The Bahamas with Sullivan Ward. Hardly believing her good fortune, Kay had the glorious premonition that it would be there, in that breathtaking island paradise, that the man she loved to distraction would at long last surrender.

Kay went from boutique to boutique searching for clothes to take on her trip. By the time the desert sun was slipping below Camelback Mountain, Kay climbed tiredly into the front seat of the borrowed Buick. The car's roomy trunk and back seat were filled with her purchases.

That evening she went out to dinner with her family and had a difficult time following the table conversation. Her mind was on Sullivan. She missed him terribly. On arising the next day she told her parents that she'd decided she really should be getting back to Denver. She was touched by the disappointment in her mother's eyes, but felt she couldn't bear one more day without seeing Sullivan.

Packing hurriedly, Kay caught the next plane to Denver. She didn't bother going to her apartment. She drove straight to the radio station, her heart speeding as she ascended to the top floor of the building. She rushed past Sherry, raising her hand to indicate she was in a hurry. Down the corridor she went, directly toward Sullivan's office.

It was empty. The top of his big desk was clean. There were no lights burning. Numbly, Kay stood staring around the room, puzzled.

"He's not here, Kay." Janelle stood in the doorway.

Kay whirled around. "No?"

"Sullivan left this morning for Vail. He went on a skiing trip. He didn't mention it to you?"

"Ah, no, I suppose he forgot." Kay smiled weakly. "How long will he stay? A couple of days?"

"Longer. He said not to look for him until after New Year's."

Kay couldn't keep from frowning. "Sullivan is going to spend New Year's in Vail with...with..."

"Alone." Janelle shook her head. "As you probably know, Q102 has a condo up there. Any of us can use it; all you have to do is sign up for the date you wish to occupy it. Sullivan looked at the records, saw no one would be using it and went up." Janelle paused, smiled understandingly at Kay and added, "He's not with a woman, Kay. I know him.

He's really alone and I've an idea he'll spend a lot of time before the fire thinking.''

"About what?"

Janelle didn't answer her question.

Seven

Promotion of the upcoming January trip to the Bahamas began on the very day Sullivan first mentioned it to Kay. The junket, a joint venture between Q102 radio and a local travel agency, was a highly advantageous form of advertising for both parties.

The popularity of the Sullivan-and-Kay morning show insured the booking of enough travelers to fill a jumbo jet to Miami. The travel agency would make a healthy profit. The radio station would receive free travel through the agency, as well as more exposure for its talented team.

Kay heard the first commercial promoting the trip driving to her apartment after learning that Sullivan was in Vail. Ace Black was on the air, and with a great deal of enthusiasm he announced to his listening audience that the "Fabulous Fly and Float Fun Package" was rapidly filling up.

Kay, grimacing at the forced alliteration, wondered who'd dreamed it up. She turned up the volume to listen to the remainder of Ace's spiel.

"For a price so modest you can't possibly pass it up, you and your mate can go on the trip of a lifetime with Sullivan and Kay acting as your hosts. Fly nonstop to Miami International where you'll board the luxury liner, *Carnivale*, for the day-long cruise to the lush, tropical island of Nassau. Spend six sun-drenched days and five flower-scented nights in the romantic..."

Kay was smiling. Six glorious days in an island paradise with Sullivan! A chill of anticipation skipped up her spine and the disappointment of Sullivan being out of town until after the first of the year began to subside. After all, in little more than three weeks, she'd have him all to herself under a Bahamian moon.

Kay laughed aloud. All to herself? Sure, with only about two hundred Denver travelers. But no matter. It would be warm and lovely and the perfect setting for romance.

Kay affixed a brand-new calendar to the door of her refrigerator with a magnetized ceramic carrot and began marking off the days. She had circled the date of January twentieth, Miami departure day, with bold red strokes. Each night before she went to bed, she marked a huge red X through the day ended and smiled like the Cheshire cat. She'd retire to snuggle beneath the warm comforter and dream of a handsome, dark, half-naked Sullivan sunning his long, lean body on beaches of soft sand while she lay beside him, sipping cooling rum drinks through a colored straw.

On the day after New Year's, Kay was in her small office at the station, her booted feet resting on her desk, the latest copy of *Billboard* magazine on her lap. She yawned, closed her eyes and laid her head back against the tall padded leather chair. She was sleepy. She just had to close her eyes for a few moments.

"We don't allow no slackers 'round here." The deep, teasing voice brought her heart-poundingly awake.

In the door, leaning lazily against the frame, stood a grinning Sullivan Ward. Not expecting him, overwhelmed by his compelling presence, Kay found herself speechless and paralyzed. Silently scolding herself for not being able to come back with some welcoming remark of her own, she remained reclining in her chair, watching him step inside, close the door and approach her.

"Sweetheart," he kidded, putting his hands to her booted feet. "Only important executives like me should be propping their feet on their desks."

Kay licked her dry lips, looking up at him. Wearing what she was certain was an idiotic smile, she nodded and watched while he gently moved her feet to the floor, took hold of her arm and pulled her up from the chair. The forgotten magazine slid from her lap. His hands were on her upper arms; he was standing very close to her and he was still smiling. "I'm awfully disappointed, Kay," he said, his eyes going to her mouth.

"Why?" She found her tongue. "Reading *Billboard* is just as important to our profession as...what?"

Sullivan Ward kissed her nose, shook his head and took her hand. "I meant, I thought you'd miss me, but you don't seem at all thrilled to see me."

"Oh, Sullivan. I am, really," she quickly assured him, thinking to herself he would never know that she'd lived for this moment since she'd left him to fly to Phoenix.

"Well, that's a little better." He dropped her hand, slid his up to lightly grip the nape of her neck and drew her to the door. "Buy me a cup of coffee and tell me all about your holiday."

They went down the hall toward the coffee room, Sullivan never releasing her neck. He stood so close to her that Kay could feel the coldness clinging to his knee-length tweed coat. But the hand upon her neck was so warm and welcome it caused a curl of fire to spread through Kay. Cheeks coloring, she vividly imagined how it would feel to have that sure, warm hand glide over her entire body.

"Damn," Sullivan was saying, "here I'm freezing and you're not the least bit chilly." He gave her a sly grin, his eyes flashing disturbingly. "Your pretty face is glowing with warmth."

Kay looked up at him, shrugged his hand away and said, "Perhaps hot coffee will do the trick. Sullivan, what is it?"

"Nothing, really, Kay. It's just—" He paused and in his eyes was the faintest hint of embarrassment. "I'm glad to see you."

"I'm glad you're glad."

Kay paced the white-carpeted floor of her apartment. She hugged herself, rubbing her arms. Sighing, she again hurried to the sliding glass door at the front of the living room. Peering out into the gathering darkness, she could see the snow was growing heavier.

Pushed by driving winds, the huge wet snowflakes swirled around, covering Kay's high balcony as well as the manicured grounds below, the city streets and the busy freeways. Kay whirled, stormed down the hall to her bedroom and again checked the neatly packed suitcases scattered all around the room.

In her frustration, Kay talked aloud to herself. "I just know we won't get to go tomorrow," she railed bleakly. "There's bound to already be six inches of snow on the ground and if it continues..."

Kay flung herself down onto her bed, picked up the television remote control and flicked on the set. Channel ten's weatherman did nothing to allay her worst fears. "The cold air mass came down from Canada." He indicated a colored map behind him. "The national weather service gives me little hope that this, the worst blizzard of the season, will end anytime soon. The mercury should dip well below the zero mark tonight, and pay no heed to that old adage 'it's too cold to snow.' It doesn't get too cold to snow and snow, which we're already having, will increase during the night. We expect anywhere from—"

Kay angrily flipped off the set. "Damn." She sighed. "Damn, damn, damn." Back to the living room she hurried, rushing once again to look out at the storm in the Rockies that was becoming a very real threat to the trip she'd looked forward to with childlike excitement.

The plane she and Sullivan were to board for the Bahamas holiday was to leave at 8:00 a.m. Today Sullivan had taken her to lunch at Leo's, where they met various members of the gang. She'd been elated when he'd turned to her and said, so softly the others didn't hear him, "How would you like a sausage pizza?"

That he would remember all these years so thrilled her. Kay became more optimistic than ever that when they reached the island, that the two of them would...

He shared the pizza with her and they laughed and lingered after the others had one by one drifted back across the street to the radio station. Alone at the long table, they slowly sipped their wine and discussed everything from politics to prayer to passion. Religion to records to romance. Food to funnypapers to flying. You name it, they talked about it. It was just the way it had been when they were falling in love the first time.

By the time Sullivan and Kay reluctantly left the deserted bar and stepped out into the street, they were met with the first dusting of small, crystal snowflakes. Neither thought much about it. It often snowed in Denver in January.

Kay stopped by Sullivan's office at five-thirty to say goodnight. "So Jeff is to pick you up, then you two will come to my place no later than seven?" Kay thrust her hands deep into the pockets of her red fox jacket.

"Seven sharp." Sullivan, nodding, rose from his chair. "Now be ready, Kay. You know we have to check in and be on board to greet the travelers."

"I'll be ready and waiting." She smiled and rubbed a cheek on the tickly soft fur of her jacket. "I'm going straight home, will do all last-minute packing, take a bath and go right to bed."

"Sounds good. Tell you what, since it's snowing, why don't you give me a call tonight. Just so I'll know you're home and safe, okay?"

"No. Not okay."

"Why?"

Kay smiled. "You call me."

"Done."

* * *

Kay's telephone rang. She jerked up the receiver. "Yes?"

"Can you believe this?" Sullivan's deep voice sounded concerned.

"Oh, Sullivan, do you think we'll get to go?"

"Kay, to be honest, I'm not so sure. I was hoping come night the storm would lighten up, but if anything, it's getting worse."

"I know," Kay said disappointedly. "I just know we won't get to go! I could cry."

"Don't do that. The thought of you crying is more than I can bear. Stapleton will have the snowplows out all night. Keep the faith."

Kay sighed. "I'll try, but I don't mind telling you I'll be terribly upset if we don't get to go."

"Tell you what, if the trip is cancelled, I'll bring a bathing suit, a sunlamp and my old Belafonte record of 'Island in the Sun' over to your place. We'll slather on oil and stretch out by the fire." His deep laughter filled her ear.

She laughed, too. "Not quite the same, Sullivan; however, I may hold you to it."

"Get some rest, Kay. Jeff and I will be by to pick you up at seven."

"Sullivan," she said, "I'll offer up a solemn little prayer if you will."

Sullivan laughed louder. "Sweetheart, let's hope the almighty has something more important on his mind than a couple of Denver disc jockeys longing to flee to warm sands to behave like pagans."

"You're right." Kay felt a twinge of guilt. "But I intend to do it just the same."

"Night, Kay," Sullivan said, still chuckling. "You pray, I'll cross my fingers."

Kay replaced the receiver, sighed again and did indeed say a silent prayer. Never had she wanted anything more than this planned trip to go off as scheduled. It wasn't just the enjoyable vacation in a beautiful locale. It was the rest of her life at stake here!

Kay tossed and turned and finally found the blessed release of sleep. The alarm jangled at 5:00 a.m. Kay's eyes flew open and she bounded from her bed, hurrying anxiously to the window. Snow, blinding white and thick, was falling as it had all night long. Drifts, five and six feet high, piled up against surrounding buildings. Streetlights were almost invisible in the relentless fast-falling snow. Kay's chest tightened with alarm.

She turned on the radio. Dale Kitrell was speaking. "and it looks as though it will keep right on falling. Accumulations of up to fourteen inches have been reported in the foothills."

Feeling as though she might cry, Kay, jerking the soft pink flannel nightgown over her head, went to the shower thinking—major airports do not close simply because of a little snowstorm. They have plows to clear runways. There's absolutely nothing for me to worry about.

She'd just exited from the shower when her phone rang. For a moment Kay, a big towel wrapped around her damp body, simply stared at it, afraid of what she'd hear. After four loud, insistent rings she jerked it up and said, "Hello."

"Kay—" Sullivan's deep voice sounded urgent "—I know it'll rush you too much, but do you suppose you could be ready to leave your place by six-fifteen? I'm afraid we're going to have a devil of a time getting to the airport."

Kay, nodding furiously, suddenly realized he couldn't see her. "Yes, yes," she almost shouted at him. "I'll be ready. Sullivan, will we get to go?"

"Don't know, but let's be there in case."

"I'll be ready."

Kay, dressed in warm wool slacks of gray and a navy pullover sweater with an oxford-cloth blouse of white underneath, threw open her front door to see Sullivan in a heavy overcoat of black, a long plaid scarf of black and white wrapped around his neck.

He gathered up her gray suede suitcases while Kay tugged on her coat, gloves and a warm wool cap. Silently they descended in the elevator where Jeff, waiting in the quiet lobby, relieved Sullivan of part of his burden, winked at Kay and said, "I felt sure you'd be wearing a sundress, C.A."

Kay rolled her eyes and hurried out the door, down the slippery front steps to the four-wheel-drive van parked at the curb, its engine idling. The men loaded her baggage in the back beside Sullivan's and Jeff climbed behind the wheel, while Kay slid in the middle, Sullivan beside her.

Jeff was whistling as though it were a lovely spring day and Kay found his good humor irritating. "Jeff, do you mind?" She shot a silencing glance at him.

His eyes twinkled. "Honey, you're worrying for nothing. By ten minutes after the hour of eight, you'll be up above all this and on your way to sunny Florida."

"Damn it, Jeff," Sullivan said, a long arm draped along the seat behind Kay, "don't go getting her hopes up. You know this is one of the worst blizzards in years." He glanced at Kay's tight face.

Kay leaned forward, turned on the radio and anxiously listened to Ace Black, filling in for them, saying, "That was some hot music for a cold morning. Word's just in that the officials are at this moment considering the closing of Stapleton International. Many flights have already been canceled and it looks as though...."

Sullivan switched off the radio. "It's out of our hands, Kay. We may get lucky and get out before the airport closes."

Jeff, expertly maneuvering the four-wheel-drive vehicle over the snow-packed streets, said cheerfully, "You know, I can't help but think there's some sort of conspiracy here, Ward. The station sends you on a promo trip and you get this sweet, beautiful girl for your traveling companion. You get to go to Nassau and stay in the Paradise Island Hotel with grand rooms, good restaurants, even casinos. The promo trip I had, I was sent to some godforsaken island where thatched-roofed huts were the only accommodations. And my traveling partner? Ace Black. If I hadn't wisely packed the Scrabble board, I'd have gone crazy. Although Ace has got to be the world's worst Scrabble player and he snores besides.''

Kay and Sullivan laughed. Sullivan could see Jeff's entertaining chatter was helping to relax a very nervous Kay. "Tell Kay about the time you went to Vegas."

"Oh, yeah—" Jeff bobbed his head "—I forgot about that one. They send Sullivan out there with a full plane about six months ago, put him up at Caesar's, naturally. You know, king-size beds, movies in your room, great shows. But me? Sure, I get a trip to Vegas. I'm put up in some off-the-Strip place called Western Sunset. Do I get a king-size bed? Uh-uh. I've a bale of hay tossed in the corner. Television? Sure. A thirteen-inch black and white. Did you know they still make black-and-white television sets? I didn't." He continued to regale Kay with tales of his less than satisfactory excursions and Kay's tinkling laughter filled the van's cab. She was still laughing when they arrived at Stapleton International Airport.

Inside the terminal, Kay's apprehension returned. Flights were canceled by all the airlines. Heart hammering, Kay's blue eyes scanned the ever-changing Eastern Airline monitor. Flight 111 for Miami was still scheduled to depart from gate ten at eight.

Jeff insisted he stay until they took off. Sullivan, looking over Kay's head at Jeff, nodded his agreement. Neither man was sure they wouldn't need a ride back home.

Kay could hardly believe it when she and Sullivan waved goodbye to Jeff. "Happy trails, kiddies." Jeff kissed Kay's cheek and shook hands with Sullivan.

She and Sullivan boarded the plane. Smiling stewards and stewardesses greeted the pair and showed them where the plane's intercom microphones were located. It had been agreed that both would say a few words of welcome to the passengers once they were airborne.

Eager travelers were soon boarding. Kay and Sullivan stood at the portal, shaking hands and welcoming them on board. In a matter of minutes every seat in the coach was full on the big jet, the doors were closed and locked and Kay and Sullivan took their seats in the first-class section.

While the heavy, blowing snows buffeted the shiny wet plane, the captain taxied out to the one runway still open and Kay, though elated that they were on their way, felt that old unease twisting at her stomach as it always did on take-off. She flew often. But she had never gotten over her illogical fear. Sullivan remembered.

"We're cleared for takeoff," came the captain's voice as the plane's engines grew deafeningly loud and he turned on full power.

"Kay," Sullivan said softly and took her cold hand. He drew it to his stomach and held it in both of his. She smiled her gratitude as they hurled headlong down the icy runway and into the air. Up, up through the thick, blinding snow they rose, until finally, to the cheers of the crowd in the cabin, the silver plane broke through to a bright, blue sky at thirty-five thousand feet.

Kay laughed, squeezed Sullivan's hand happily and said, "I worried for nothing."

"That's right," he agreed, flipped open his seat belt and said, "let's go to the mikes and say a few words."

Jeff Kerns, making his way back to the radio station, heard the news just as he was leaving the airport entrance. "Stapleton International Airport is now officially closed."

Eastern's flight 111 was the very last to get off the ground.

Sullivan and Kay were in high spirits upon landing at Miami International. They, along with their happy Denver travelers, climbed aboard waiting motor coaches for the journey to the pier where the sleek, impressive cruise ship stood gleaming white in the warm Florida sun.

Kay, her face awash with pleasure, clung to Sullivan's hand and hurried up onto the sun deck, saying happily, "As soon as we wave goodbye, I'm going to get out of these hot clothes!"

Sullivan smiled indulgently. "Why wait? It'll be a good half hour before we hoist anchor."

"But our baggage, will it be—"

"It'll be in your stateroom by the time you get there."

"Help me find my compartment?"

Sullivan chuckled. "Gladly. It's next door to mine." Sullivan led Kay down two levels to the promenade deck, where the prized deluxe outside staterooms were located. He accompanied her into the plush room and enjoyed the look of delight on her face when, her eyes sweeping the red and white interior with its shining glass window offering an unobstructed view of the sea, she poked her head into the bath and whirled.

"Sullivan! There's even a tub." Before he could answer, she was jerking the card from a bon-voyage basket of fruit. "How sweet," she said. "It's from the entire staff of Q102." She lowered the card and saw them. A dozen Happiness roses rested in a water-filled crystal vase on the night table by her bed. Kay looked nervously at Sullivan, afraid to assume anything. He was looking at her but the mysterious depths of his eyes gave nothing away.

Kay walked to the roses, read the card and leaned forward to inhale of the roses' sweet fragrance. She slowly turned around and saw that Sullivan was smiling at her. "Thank you," she said softly, walked to him and put a hand to his strong jaw. She stood on tiptoe and gave his smooth cheek a kiss. He seemed neither pleased nor perplexed.

"Meet you topside in fifteen minutes." He turned and left her.

Kay stripped off the hot sweater the minute he closed the door. She liked the look that came into his eyes when she joined him at the ship's railing. She liked even better the feel of a long arm coming around her waist to draw her close to him. They stood high above the pier, waving to the crowd below, and Kay threw back her head and laughed when the big, sleek ship began to maneuver out of the bay toward the open Atlantic.

"You should try to cheer up, Kay," Sullivan kidded, and Kay laughed all the harder. Sullivan laughed with her. Kay was sure it was going to be a glorious trip.

Moonlight shimmered on the ocean as Sullivan and Kay languidly strolled around the polished promenade deck, smiling and nodding to members of their group reclining in deck chairs or taking the sea breeze after dinner.

In the distance, a million twinkling lights were steadily growing closer. Passengers soon lined the smooth railing as the port of Nassau came up to meet them. Everyone went ashore and Kay, riding across the island, peered out the window at the lush green-black foliage enveloping the narrow route.

Over the bridge the rattling taxi sped, to Paradise Island, where the group's hotel rooms awaited them. Yawning behind her hand and promising herself she'd see everything come morning, Kay willingly let Sullivan guide her past the bustling casino to her room on the top floor of the hotel. A smiling bellman led the way, loaded down with baggage.

Sullivan bid her good-night and Kay, briefly studying the lovely room of green and white, crossed to the closed white-slatted double doors and flung them open. Bright moonlight streamed into the room and the sound of the breakers crashing against the beach made Kay realize she truly had arrived at this Caribbean Shangri-la.

Kay inhaled deeply of the sweet night air, turned and undressed for bed. The last thought before she lost consciousness was, "It is Tuesday night. We leave the island on Monday morning. I have five days and five nights to make Sullivan see that we are made for each other." She was smiling as she fell asleep.

It was a wonderful but busy time for Kay and the Denver crowd. Her role as hostess made it necessary for her to escort some of the travelers across the island bridge for shopping and browsing. The fashionable shops of Bay Street were a delight, and only a couple of blocks away, the world's largest straw market was a favorite of the Denverites. Kay bought a wide-brimmed hat to wear through the narrow streets.

She took a tour through the residential sections, admiring the colorful white and pink colonial houses, products of the island's British influence. She lunched with some of the group at quaint little outdoor cafés and joined them for games of backgammon in the cheerful sun room at the hotel.

It was all enjoyable, but Kay would have preferred spending her time with Sullivan. Sullivan was busy also. He accompanied some of the tourists on fishing excursions, he played gin rummy in organized tournaments, he went for sunrise swims in the surf with the athletic members of the group.

Still, Sullivan and Kay did find time to be together. It was mid-afternoon on Thursday that Kay, breaking away from the tired people she'd spent the morning and noontime with, donned a pale blue bikini, drew on an ankle-length cover-up and headed for the beach.

Kay walked determinedly past the hotel pool with its row upon row of padded chaise longues holding vacationers of every size and shape, all with varying degrees of tans. Kay idly wondered why anyone would come to this glorious island and choose to lie by the pool when the beach lay not fifty yards away.

Shrugging slender shoulders and silently deciding, "to each his own," Kay crossed the heated red cement beside the huge pool, went down a set of iron stairs and smiled happily. Before her the emerald-green Caribbean washed up onto the sugary-white sands of the beach. Tall, swaying palms offered scant shade for the weakhearted, while overhead the bright Bahamian sun beat down, turning the blue-green water to blinding pools of light as far as the eye could see.

Kay walked barefooted along the powdery hot sand, choosing just the right place to spread her beach towel. Hurriedly shedding the lace cover-up, Kay stretched out on her back, squinted up into the sun, sighed and closed her eyes. She was almost dozing, the heat of the sun draining the energy from her exposed body, when a shadow fell between her and the sun.

Kay's eyes fluttered open to see Sullivan standing above her. Making no effort to hide his assessing perusal of her, his dark eyes slid slowly up her long, slender legs to the gentle curve of her hips and her bare flat stomach. The intense gaze moved to the full, ripe breasts skimpily covered with the pale-blue bikini bra. Kay felt her already heated body grow warmer still under his unwavering appraisal.

It was not her lack of clothing alone that made her feel faint and flushed. Sullivan wore only a pair of black, quick-drying nylon swim trunks, and the manly vision he projected standing above her with his bare feet apart was enough to heat any woman's blood. The shoulders, wet from the sea, fairly shimmered in the sun's harsh rays. Beads of water glistened in the thatch of black hair covering his chest. Long legs, as tanned as his chest and arms, looked strong and powerful. The blatant masculinity hinted at beneath his clothes was all too boldly displayed in the short, snug swim trunks.

Sullivan, dropping to his knees beside her, said thickly, "Aren't you afraid you'll burn completely up?"

"As a matter of fact, I am." She smiled at him, thinking it was he, not the sun, that was threatening to incinerate her.

Sullivan stretched out on his side near her, weight supported on an elbow. His eyes went wistfully out to where sky met sea, but Kay saw the clenching of his jaw and knew he was just as susceptible to her as she was to him. If only he would admit it.

They lay out until sundown. Then it was time to dress for the cocktail party they were hosting at poolside. Kay chose a simple sundress of beige linen and saw that her shoulders were turning pink from the day's afternoon at the beach. Longing for the kind of tan she'd had in the summer, she promised herself she'd somehow find more time to sunbathe.

The days and the nights were flying past much too fast. Kay was having a glorious time, and Sullivan, she had to admit, spent as much time as he could with her. It was hardly his fault that there were so many planned activities that they had to take part in. Every day's agenda was crammed with obligations for both of them.

Except Sunday.

That was to be an entirely free day for the tired, happy travelers.

Saturday night rolled around and Kay, her slim body browned by the hot Bahamian sun, dressed for the dinner dance she and Sullivan were to host in the elegant ballroom. Kay stepped from the tub and patted her body dry, fighting the sinking, sad feeling she'd been experiencing all afternoon. How could it have all gone by so fast? And how could she have spent all this time in one of the most beautifully romantic spots in the entire universe and with the only man she would ever want and not have elicited so much as a good-night kiss from him?

Kay sighed, tossed the towel aside and slipped on a pair of silky panty hose. From the closet she took the new, slinky white crepe dress, slipped it over her head and hooked the halter-type top in back of her neck. Turning to the mirror, she evaluated herself with objectivity. The dress, completely backless, zipped from midhip to waist. Her slender back, with its newly acquired tan, curved gracefully. Her hips gently flared and the long dress fell to the floor in soft swaying folds. Braless breasts pushed provocatively against the lush fabric covering them. Kay nodded her approval and opened an expensive bottle of perfume she'd purchased at one of the duty-free shops. She tipped the small vial up to a forefinger and let that finger go into the shadowy valley between her breasts. A dab inside each elbow, and Kay stoppered the bottle and set it back in its place.

She grabbed a brush and gave her hair one last vigorous stroking, letting it swirl around her tanned bare shoulders. "Sullivan," she said into the mirror, "it's now or never!"

A string orchestra was on a stage in the marble-floored ballroom. They were tuning up in the still-empty room; strange chords filling the room where red-jacketed waiters were busy depositing glasses of ice water, silver bowls with pats of butter resting atop crushed ice and silver salt and pepper shakers on round white-clothed tables lining the dance floor.

"Am I late?" came the velvet voice from behind her.

Kay turned. Sullivan, elegantly handsome in a tuxedo as black as his hair, was smiling at her. Lean fingers worried his black bow tie. The stiff French cuffs of his cloud-white shirt were set off with onyx links.

"No, I'm early." Kay brushed his hand aside, reaching up to straighten the worrisome tie.

"Thanks," Sullivan said, jutting his left wrist out from under the shirt's cuff for a glance at his gold watch. "You're right, it's just now 8:30 p.m."

Every member of the happy Denver group attended the dinner dance, all dressed in their finest, laughing, talking, finding they'd made close friends here in this island paradise with people who'd lived in the same city with them for a lifetime.

Sullivan and Kay dined at the head table with eight travelers who considered themselves extremely lucky to be the table companions of their charming hosts. Before the last of the diners had finished with their dessert, couples drifted to the dance floor. Kay, eagerly anticipating being swept around the big room in Sullivan's arms, shot a daggerlike look at the brazen redhead who came to tap him on the shoulder, bat her long eyelashes at him and say in a voice filled with honey, "Sullivan, I'm just dying to dance with you. My girlfriend—" she nodded toward a smiling brunette two tables away "—bet me I didn't have the nerve to come over and ask you." She smiled prettily and leaned so close to him, Kay was unable to see his face or hear his reply.

The answer was clear enough when the woman giggled happily, straightened and stepped back. Sullivan pushed back his chair and guided the redhead to the floor. The smitten woman lifted a bare arm around his neck and pressed herself so close to him that Sullivan colored visibly. Kay, her blue eyes turning green, watched intently while the swaying couple moved around the room. The woman's eyes were closed in ecstasy.

Relieved when the song ended, Kay bit the inside of her lip in frustration when she saw the pair walking to where the brunette girlfriend was seated. Sullivan was speaking, and the woman got up, tugged on his arm and dragged him onto the floor while her redheaded friend dropped down into her chair and took a big sip of wine.

So went the evening. It wasn't Sullivan's fault. Kay knew that. In fact, she, too, found herself being pursued and spun around the polished floor in the eager arms of more than one boisterous male who was intent on having a grand time. Sullivan gave Kay knowing looks when their eyes met as they graciously danced in the arms of the partyers.

It was nearing midnight before Kay, her feet beginning to swell in the silver high-heeled sandals, smiled gratefully and stepped into the commanding arms of Sullivan Ward.

"Tell you what," he whispered near her ear, "when this song ends, you slowly, but surely, make your way toward the door. I'll follow in exactly five minutes. They'll never know we're gone."

"I'll be in the casino by the first row of slot machines," she murmured, and felt all the listlessness leave her body.

Neither spoke for the remainder of the dance. The orchestra was playing an old romantic ballad and a smooth-voiced, young black Bahamian was singing. The roomful of chattering, laughing people faded away and there were only the two of them, moving as one, swaying around the floor. Sullivan held her very close. She was tingling from his nearness. His hard chest and muscled thighs were pressing against her and his hand upon her bare, sensitive back was spread, the tips of his fingers like fire upon her cool skin.

Kay would have sworn that his smooth, warm lips were scattering tiny little kisses on the wispy hair beside her temples. A slow, spreading coil of desire began to build in her lower stomach, pleasantly stirring sleeping pulses throughout her body. Kay closed her eyes and wondered if it were possible to actually die from wanting someone too much.

Shaken by the emotions the romantic dance had evoked, Kay felt Sullivan's breath against her hair. "Okay, carry out our plan."

She could only nod as he released her. In a daze, she sidled out of the ballroom, down the carpeted corridor and into the lively casino. Stopping at the row of slot machines where she'd told Sullivan she'd meet him, Kay leaned against one of the tall one-armed bandits and cast her attention to a dice table twenty feet away.

Drawn by the shouting, excited players standing around the big, green felt table, Kay walked over, took some bills from her evening bag and bought some five-dollar chips. She dropped one on the pass line and squealed when, on the come out, the shooter, a short, stocky man with a cigar clamped firmly between his teeth, tossed the red dice the length of the table and they rolled over onto eleven.

Childishly clapping her hands, Kay picked up her won money, leaving the original chip. A charming, British tuxedoed croupier standing to her right turned toward her and said softly, "Not only beautiful, but lucky, too, sweetheart?" His green eyes flashed at her, and he added very quietly, "I get off at 4:00 a.m."

"Good for you." Sullivan's deep voice sounded clipped. Stepping in between Kay and the croupier, he said possessively, "'Sweetheart' here will be in bed long before then." He took Kay's elbow and drew her away from the table.

Kay loved Sullivan's obvious flash of jealousy, but said, "My money, Sullivan. I've got five dollars riding on the pass line."

"I'll reimburse you." He looked pointedly at the impudent croupier. "If she wins, the take's yours. It's all you'll ever get from her, understand?"

His features hard, Sullivan guided Kay through the busy casino and out a pair of French doors at the side. Down marbled steps and into a tropical garden they strolled, the full moon lighting the lush, manicured grounds.

His hand was holding her upper arm and he continued to walk her farther from the hotel, past the lighted empty swimming pool, down more steps and to the beach.

Finally he spoke. "Let's walk on the beach."

"I'd love to," Kay said and immediately amended, "but I can't, I'll get sand in my shoes."

"Take 'em off."

"It's not just the shoes, Sullivan, what about my hose?"

Sullivan unbuttoned his jacket and thrust a hand into his pocket. "So take them off, too."

"But they're pantyhose and I'm not wearing—that is—" Kay felt herself blushing hotly.

"Look around you, Kay. There's no one on the beach. I'll turn my back. You slip out of your pantyhose and we'll walk along the sand in the moonlight." The tightness had left his mouth and he was smiling.

"Turn around," she said, handing him her shoes. Sullivan, the shoes over a thumb, turned away from her, looking out over the restless sea. Kay, nervously casting worried eyes all around her, slid the silky pantyhose down over her hips and legs, hopping on one foot to take them off. Letting her skirt drop, she stood with the wadded hose in her hands and felt dangerously exposed. She wore nothing but the white crepe dress, and the breeze coming in off the ocean gently molded the filmy dress to her slender body.

Debating already how she could get back to her hotel room without relinquishing all modesty, Kay heard Sullivan say, exasperated, "I could have undressed completely by now." He turned around, saw the strained look on her pretty face and assured her, "Kay, you will not see anyone tonight." He took the hose and stuffed them in his suit pocket. "When we get back to the hotel, we'll use the entrance nearest your room and I'll run interference for you, so relax."

She did. It was a gorgeous, perfect night. Waves crashed in on the shore with lulling repetition. The moon turned the white sands to crystals of shiny silver. Soft, tickling breezes lifted strands of Kay's long, feathered hair, making her raise her free hand to push it from her eyes. The other small hand was held securely in Sullivan's.

They walked for a long way down the deserted beach, talking little, drinking in the beauty surrounding them, enjoying each other's company and the unspoken closeness between them. Kay felt her heart lurch with happiness when finally Sullivan said, "It's time we go in."

"Yes," she said breathlessly, the soft, filmy dress, driven by the night winds, caressing her naked body, arousing her, teasing at flesh that craved the tall, dark man beside her.

They were at the door of her hotel room. Kay fumbled with the key, eager to open the portal to complete bliss. She turned and looked expectantly up at Sullivan, dropping the key back into her evening bag. Sullivan picked up her hand, raised it to his lips and kissed the warm palm.

"Kay." His voice was husky.

"Yes?" Hers was breathless.

"Good night," he said. And handing her the silver shoes, he turned and walked away.

Eight

Stunned and unbelieving, Kay stood motionless, feeling her stomach knot painfully beneath the soft crepe of her evening dress. Hand cold and stiff, she slowly closed the door, dropped the shoes and valiantly fought back the sob welling up in her throat. She crossed the floor to the opposite side of the room.

Kay drew open the slatted double doors leading onto the private balcony that overlooked the white sand beach and the restless sea beyond. She stepped, barefooted, out onto the high balcony and made no effort to lift her hand when flower-scented breezes tossed her long, loose hair into her face. Kay stood alone in the moonlight, her slender body trembling with need. Tears of hurt and pain stung at the backs of her eyes.

The breeze off the ocean was cool. It gently stroked her, as though generously offering its soothing, healing help to the sad young woman clinging to the iron-lace railing, her body afire, her longing a real and painful ache, her frustration and heartache unbearable.

Kay whirled and went back inside, anxiously stripping the soft dress from her heated body. She turned on no lamps. None were necessary. Through the open balcony doors moonlight sliced the big room exactly in half. The room's bed, its covers turned down by the maid, rested half in, half out of the penetrating light. While the fluffy pillows at the headboard were barely visible in the dark shadows, the lower portion of the bed with its folded-back white sheets lay in silvery light as bright as day.

It was the darkness that Kay sought. Tears now sliding down her cheeks, she stood in the shadows and discarded the beautiful white dress, letting it slide down her naked breasts and hips to the floor, discarding it along with her dreams. Ignoring the yellow knee-length terry-cloth robe draped across the foot of the bed, Kay walked into the adjoining bath, snatching a plastic shower cap from the hook by the mirrored medicine cabinet.

Hastily shoving her hair up under the cap, caring little that a few heavy strands remained clinging to her neck, unprotected, she stepped into the shower, jerked the curtains closed and twirled the cold-water faucet full open. Cold, pelting water hissed upon bare, heated flesh.

It did little good.

When Kay stepped from the cold shower ten minutes later, her body temperature may have been a little lower, but the clawing need deep in her stomach remained. She was listlessly patting at her wet body when she heard the soft knock on her door. Sudden confusion mixed with panic and hope. Body still damp, Kay grabbed for the robe while the knock came once again.

"I'm coming," she said, heart pounding in her chest, and rushed to the door. She was turning the knob when she remembered she still wore the drenched shower cap. She pulled it from her head, rushed to drop it in the lavatory and realized in despair that her long hair lay in damp, untidy disarray around her shiny face.

Running nervous fingers through the tangled mane, she lowered her hands, jerked frantically at the sash of her robe, took a shallow breath and said, "Who is it?"

"Sullivan," was the firm, one-word response.

Stifling a gasp, Kay opened the door.

He stood there, raised hands clasping either side of the door frame. The elegantly tailored tuxedo jacket was gone. The white shirt was unbuttoned down his chest, the long tail hanging outside his trousers, sleeves rolled up over his arms. His feet were bare. Unruly black hair looked as though a nervous male hand had been raking repeatedly through it.

Sullivan said nothing. One hand finally left the door-jamb, went to his pants pocket and brought out a pair of silky pantyhose. He slowly held them out toward her.

"Oh," Kay said, looking up at his dark, unreadable face. "Thank you. I . . . I forgot." She lifted her hand, took the hose and automatically moved a step backward, pulling the door completely open.

For an interminable time, Sullivan stood there in the doorway, saying nothing, his burning eyes devouring her.

"Kay," he finally managed, and it was no more than a strangled whisper.

"Yes, Sullivan?" She held her breath.

He moved into the room. He closed the door behind him, his eyes never leaving her. "Kay, I . . . I hurt. I hurt so bad, baby. Help me. Hold me."

A flood of love and happiness washed over her as she murmured softly, "Oh, my darling," and stepped into his embrace, flinging her protective, eager arms up around the strong column of his neck.

Sullivan leaned to her and his arms enclosed her, desperately pressing her warm, willing body up to his tall, hard length. "Love me, honey. Please, love me. Kay," he gasped thickly against her sweet-smelling damp hair.

"Dear God," Kay marveled aloud in muffled awe against his shoulder. "You care. Sul, you still care."

"I said I'd care forever—" he slid a lean hand up to cradle her head, gently pulling it back so that he could look at her "—and I meant forever, Kay." His eyes were filled with love and desire.

"My Sul." She looked up at him, her blue shining eyes mirroring her happiness and relief.

"Kiss me, Kay. Kiss away all my pain. Love me."

His mouth slowly descended to hers. Kay watched not his mouth, but his eyes, as warm, parted lips gently settled on hers. She shivered as she saw those dark eyes closing in ecstasy, the long, sweeping lashes fluttering down to tickle her sensitive cheeks. Then her eyes also closed as she surrendered totally to the masterful mouth moving hungrily upon hers.

Sullivan was gently nipping at the soft flesh inside her bottom lip, teeth raking playfully, before he sucked the lip into his mouth for an instant. He released it, kissed the left corner of her open lips and said against her cheek, "Kay, sweet, I want to kiss you all night long. I want to kiss you enough to make up for all the years I starved for the taste of you."

His mouth moved back to hers, his tongue sweeping across her small, even teeth, then sliding into the darkness behind them. Kay clung to his neck and let the warmth in her body and his rise unchecked while his hot tongue explored the tingling, sensitive inside of her open mouth. It was his to invade, his to claim, his to taste and drink from.

Sullivan did just that. His lips, teeth and tongue possessed the sweet, dark cavern of her mouth. He took his time, intent on drawing all the honey from her, feeding ravenously on the sweetness he was starving for, could not get enough of, could no longer live without.

When at last his mouth reluctantly separated from hers, Sullivan lifted a hand to push aside the scratchy terry robe's lapel from Kay's left shoulder. He lowered his burning lips to the gentle curve of her neck and shoulder, kissing the warm, clean flesh.

Nibbling there, he murmured huskily, "Oh, Kay, my only love, I want to kiss you all night and all over." Gently he bit her neck. "I want to kiss your nipples and your navel and your knees." His open lips pressed ever hotter caresses to the side of her throat while she trembled happily against him and felt she would surely burst into flames from his words as well as his kisses.

Sullivan lifted his head. "And I want you to kiss me, too, baby. I want your gleaming little mouth to claim mine, to drive me wild as only you know how. Will you do that for me?"

Kay, her hands locked behind his head, pantyhose still clutched tightly in slim fingers, said breathlessly, "Lower your head and I'll show you."

Sullivan eagerly bent his head as Kay stood on tiptoe and began slowly, teasingly kissing his full mouth. Her lips played with his, nibbling, licking, withdrawing, finally twisting provocatively. Kay ran the tip of her tongue along the inside of his upper lip and Sullivan sighed into her mouth and pressed her closer, his hands spreading on her robed back.

She made him wait no longer. Kay opened her mouth wide and brazenly darted her tongue deep into his mouth. She felt him shudder against her and felt powerful and happy and grateful all at the same time. She explored and savored just as he had done and swayed contentedly against him when his tongue met and mated with hers.

They continued to stand there kissing in the moonlight, their breath growing increasingly labored and loud, their bodies growing hotter and hungrier. Sullivan's mouth never left Kay's, but he gently pulled her arms from around his neck, took the pantyhose from her clenched fingers and dropped them to the carpet. He placed her empty hand inside his open shirt, directly over his hammering heart. The feel of his warm, hair-covered flesh beneath her hand added new fire to Kay's burning body and she wrenched her mouth from his and began to frantically shove the white, rumpled shirt down from his wide shoulders, over his long arms and off.

Inflamed by the sight and scent of him, Kay, her blue eyes glazing, leaned to him and began to press heated lips to the broad, dark chest, murmuring, "I want to kiss you all over, too, Sul. All over, all over."

"Yes, my darling," he was saying from over her head while his hands worked at the stubborn knotted sash of her terry robe. Kay let him handle it expertly. Never bothering to disturb her obsessive kissing of his wide, hair-roughened chest, Sullivan deftly managed to maneuver one slender arm, then the other, from the robe. So caught up was Kay with the hard male chest she was busily caressing, she hardly knew when the robe slipped away.

Suddenly she became very aware of her nudity. Sullivan's warm, sure hands were pressing her close, his fingertips gliding down her naked spine to the small of her back. Kay's lips lifted from his chest and she looked up at him.

"I love you, Kay Clark," he said and pulled her closer. Thick, black curly hair tickled the full, swelling breasts he'd exposed. The contact was warm and wonderful. Kay's already tingling, tautened nipples responded instantly to the feel of the strong male chest, pleasantly abrasive, rubbing against her as Sullivan kissed her once again.

Kay stood naked against the man she loved and kissed him and kissed him and was never quite certain how they arrived at the bed. Did they walk to it? Did Sullivan carry her? She couldn't recall. She knew only that her head now rested on the soft, fat pillows in the darkness and that the sheets were cool and clean beneath her bare, hot body.

Sullivan was stretched out beside her, his handsome face barely visible above hers in the darkness. A long, heavy leg was resting over her own; she could feel the smooth, slick fabric of his pants against her naked thighs and wondered fleetingly why he still had them on.

"Kay," he was saying, a hand raking through her hair, "there's not been one week, one day, one hour that I did not miss you."

"It's been the same for me, Sul. I swear it."

"Has it, sweet?" His lips were scattering worshipful kisses over her flushed cheeks, her damp temples, her quivering chin, her fluttering eyelids. "Say it then, Kay. Say you love me. Tell me, please." A lean hand moved down to caress a swelling, ripe breast.

"Sul, I love you. I have always loved you and always will. I belong to you, now and forever."

The hand at her breast tightened upon tender flesh. A finger circled the tight little crest and Kay sighed with pleasure. "Oh, honey," he whispered in the darkness, "I love you, too. So much. So much I . . ." His hand released the breast and moved down to her narrow waist as his mouth again took hers in a deep, drugging kiss.

While the fingers of one hand tangled in her long hair, holding her mouth to his, the other hand continued to glide tenderly down her body, slipping around a bare hip, fingers spreading upon the soft rounded cheek of her bare bottom. He shifted, pressing her closer to him, letting her feel the throbbing heat behind his zipper, while his tongue went deep into her mouth and his chest pressed heavily upon her breasts.

For a long while they stayed in that position, taunting each other, pleasuring each other, savoring every magical, mystical step on the erotic road to fulfillment. Into each other's mouths they murmured love words.

Sullivan lifted his head. His eyes flashed at Kay and he pulled from her embrace. Kay watched, enraptured as he rose from the bed. She heard the zipper slide down, squinted to see as he took off his dark tuxedo pants and tossed them over a chair. He was only a large, shadowy figure; Kay could make out little save the powerful contours of his strong, male body: the chiseled, wide shoulders, the flat belly, the long legs.

The moonlight that slashed into the room covered only the lower half of the bed. Sullivan was undressing by the head of the bed. Kay's eyes stayed on him and she guiltily wished that he'd move down into the light. Kay glanced down the length of the bed. Only her slim legs shown in the moonlight, sliced off midway up her thighs.

"Kay." His velvety voice was very deep and loving.

"Yes?" She squinted back in his direction.

Sullivan's arm came out of the darkness. He reached for and found her hand. Gently he pulled her up to kneel on the bed. Kay, her entire body now awash in the moonlight, breathed shallowly, sat back on her heels and saw Sullivan step out of the darkness and into the light. He placed a bent knee on the bed behind her, leaned down and gave her mouth a kiss. When their lips separated, he put a hand to the silvery crown of her head and gently pulled it against his chest. He let her head rest there for a time while he bent over her, kissing the silky hair atop her head.

Sullivan did it for a reason. Kay took advantage of it, just as he'd intended.

Above her head he was saying softly, "Kay, I'm going to turn you so that we will be lying with our heads at the foot of the bed."

Kay, slowly tearing her curious, wide eyes away from the throbbing rod of heat that so fascinated her, tipped her head back to look questioningly up into his dark, smoldering eyes. Sullivan could read her puzzlement.

"Because, darling," he said softly, a hand cupping her cheek, "if we lie with our heads on the pillows, I won't be able to see you." His head slowly bent to her and Kay moaned deep in her throat when a warm, soothing mouth closed over her aching right nipple. Sullivan circled the little peak with his tongue, raked sharp teeth over it and finally gently sucked on it for one sweet, heart-stopping minute.

When he lifted his head, his hand took the place of his mouth as his explanation continued, his voice heavy with desire. "Kay, when I make love to you . . . when I take you, I want you to be looking into my eyes," He smiled at her. "I want to see the pain and the pleasure and the love in your dazzling blue eyes when you feel me enter you." Sullivan brushed his lips to her open mouth and gently maneuvered her down once more onto the bed, on her back, her face awash in the light of the moon, long silvery hair spread out around her fragile face. "There," he said, pleased, "isn't that better?"

Loving him completely, longing to please him in every possible way, Kay nodded dreamily. "My darling Sul," she whispered and lifted a slim hand to his dark head as he stretched out by her. "I promise to keep my eyes open wide if that is what you want."

"Kay, sweet, sweet Kay," he said thickly and let his hand glide slowly down from a full, rounded breast, over delicate ribs to her narrow waist. Fingers hesitated, spreading briefly over the flat, female stomach, its texture of smooth, warm satin. "God, you're a beauty," he said, his dark eyes watching with pleasure the quivering belly his hands were awakening. "You know," he said thoughtfully, "you're all tanned except for a lovely white strip across your full sweet breasts and your lower hips and thighs. It seems hardly fair that the most beautiful parts of your body are denied the caresses of the sun."

Kay sighed happily. "I'm afraid nude sunbathing would be frowned on even in the islands."

Sullivan, his hand moving lower, murmured, "We'll see," and bent to kiss each pearly white breast in turn while his hand possessively closed over the silvery triangle of curls between her legs. He gently urged her satiny thighs apart and Kay moaned softly and tossed her head to one side, whispering his name.

Silky female flesh, wet from wanting, was his to claim, to caress, to make his own. Gratefully, and with awe close to reverence, Sullivan's hand tenderly accepted that which was lovingly offered and he, too, moaned, beholding the sweet, angelic face of the only woman he had ever loved.

Sullivan agilely shifted, moving his long, lean body between her parted legs. He was over her now, looking down at her, weight partially resting on her. His mouth dipped to hers for a searing kiss of unrestrained passion and into her mouth he said, "I love you, Kay; never stopped, couldn't. Make me whole again, baby."

"I will, my love," she said with assurance, putting her small hands to his wide shoulders and looking directly up into his dark eyes while he lifted her hips to him and slid into her with a deep, sure thrust of his powerful male body.

It hurt very much like it did that first time, but Kay, her eyes wide open, looking into Sullivan's, bit the inside of her lip and felt the pain turning to pleasure, while above her, his breath warm upon her face, Sullivan murmured soothingly, "My love. I'm sorry, I'll stop, I'll wait."

"No," she sighed, her tight little body gripping him, sheathing him, loving him. "I want it. I want you to love me."

Sullivan sprinkled kisses over her cheeks and shoulders and breasts and felt her soft body slowly begin to relax and mold itself to his. Fleetingly wondering why there was pain for her, pain almost as intense as that night so long ago when she'd been a virgin, he let it slip from his mind as logical thought took flight and there was only his beautiful, silver-haired love moving provocatively beneath him, looking into his eyes, lifting her lovely head to press kisses into his throat, over his jaws, along his shoulders.

His passions flaring white-hot, Sullivan began to rotate his hips, driving deeper and deeper into the warm, moist sweetness holding him so tightly. His hands were clutching her hips. He was lifting her to him as their rhythm increased and they moved gloriously together.

Amidst the glowing moonlight bathing their naked entwined bodies, Sullivan and Kay ascended to a height of rapture both had long since forgotten could exist here on earth.

But they were no longer on the earth.

They were one, joined in body and spirit, soaring high among the puffy white clouds of a nirvana of their own creation, finally exploding together with a magnitude of unearthly fulfillment, shooting heavenly sparks of light and love all around them. At the very pinnacle of pleasure, Kay's eyes widened with wonder, then slowly, languidly closed. They fluttered nervously open once again until she heard her gallant lover saying, "My darling, close your eyes if you wish. I love you, Kay, I love you."

Kay smiled lazily, let her eyes close and sighed with peace when she felt Sullivan's smooth lips tenderly kissing her closed eyelids. She lay completely limp and satiated while his mouth moved worshipfully over her face, her hair, her throat, and he remained still buried inside her; she was reluctant ever to have his flesh parted from hers. His lips brushing a now-soft rosy nipple, Sullivan sighed and moved to her side, drawing her to him.

"In all of my dreams," he whispered honestly against her damp temple, "in all the times I've lain in my bed and envisioned you in my arms again, never could I have hoped it would be this sweet, this glorious, this complete."

Kay smiled, lifted a tired hand up to his full mouth to trace his sculpted lips. "I know," she said. "Sullivan, I want to tell you something."

Sullivan kissed the fingers playing along his bottom lip. "What, sweet?"

"You know, darling, that first time. That night in the Brown Palace, I was a virgin, remember?"

Sullivan pressed her closer. "Sweetheart, do you think I could ever forget?"

"Well, what I wanted to say is...I...Sul, since that night...that was the only time. There's never been...I haven't—"

Sullivan raised up on an elbow. "My sweet Kay," he said, awed, "that's why it hurt you again. Oh, honey, I hurt you; I knew it was hurting you and it's because—" The words choked off in his throat and he leaned to her, kissing her lips with exquisite gentleness. "Kay," he said, stroking a soft, silvery lock of hair back from her cheek, "it was a wonderful gift you gave me all those years ago. It was the same wonderful gift you gave me tonight. You are a treasure and you make me so happy, Kay." He chewed the inside of his jaw for a second and confessed, "Listen to me. I've been to bed with other women; had sex, but I swear to you, I've not made love since that night you left me." He saw no look of censure in her lovely eyes and he smiled, recalling her so haughtily informing him there was a difference between sex and making love. "There's a big difference, you know." He smiled and held his breath.

Kay, remembering, grinned. "Yes, I know."

Sullivan, relieved, lay back down and Kay, turning over onto her stomach, cradled a cheek in one hand; the other went to the thick, dark hair covering Sullivan's chest. Her fingertips played there, enjoying the feel of crisp, crinkly hair and warm, hard muscle underneath.

"Sul, can we talk now?"

Sullivan yawned contentedly, folded his hands beneath his head. "Yes, now we can talk, Kay, Now we can."

* * *

"Those first few months after I left I wrote to you all the time," Kay reminded him.

"Yes, and your letters were full of all the exciting things going on at your L.A. station and of your success." Sullivan pulled a pack of cigarettes from his discarded white shirt, lit one and lay back down.

"I know, but in every letter I always told you how much I missed you."

"Darling, you may have missed me, but you didn't come back to Denver on a visit for almost three months."

"I couldn't get away sooner. And what difference did it make? When I did come back, you were conveniently unavailable. Lord, I couldn't believe it, they told me you'd gone on a fishing trip in the mountains. No one knew just where."

Sullivan grinned sheepishly. "I was really holed up in my apartment."

"Sul!"

"I'm sorry, baby." He crushed out his cigarette, drew her into the circle of his long arms and let his fingers trace the high bones of her cheeks. "It was cowardly, I know, but I just couldn't see you. I was hurt and unyielding."

"I knew you'd disappeared because you didn't want to see me." Kay captured his hand, pulled it to her mouth and traced the lifeline with her tongue. "That's why I quit writing after I returned to the coast. Then, Mom and Dad moved that summer to Florida and there was no longer a reason for me to come back to Denver when I knew you wouldn't see me." She released his hand and Sullivan moved it down to cup her bare shoulder.

"I came to L.A. once," he admitted almost shyly.

"Sullivan?" Kay raised up on an elbow. "When? Did you try to see me, call me?"

"I did see you."

"I don't . . . you . . ."

Sullivan sighed. "Honey, I meant to call you and take you out to dinner. Then I lost my nerve, but they were having a big parade and I fought the children and their indignant parents for a front-row spot on the sidewalk of Sunset Boulevard, because I'd heard your radio station had a float in the parade.''

"That's how you knew—" Kay's blue eyes widened.

Sullivan nodded and smiled up at her. "There you were, showing off all your best assets to a panting crowd, while I stood, my blood boiling, hating you, loving you." His smile faded. "God, I wanted to jerk you off that float, cover you with my shirt and drag you home."

"Darling," Kay said softly, "why didn't you?"

"Kay, sweetheart, I've a feeling you would have kicked my shins and told me to mind my own damn business, and you'd have been right. You're a grown woman, capable of making your own decisions without any help from me. I knew that from the time you left me; that's what hurt so much. I wanted you to be my sweet, adoring little Kay. You wanted a lot more and I don't blame you."

"Sullivan, you're so wise, you always were." Kay toyed with a lock of hair falling over his forehead. "You let me go. You knew I was making a mistake and yet—"

"Hold on, Kay," he interrupted. "I didn't think it was a mistake. I still don't. You've as much right to choose which road to travel as—"

"I chose the wrong one, darling. I've wasted years I could have been in your arms, so let's waste no more." Kay leaned down, gave his mouth a soft, sweet kiss and murmured against his lips, "Teach me, Sul. Show me how to be your lover."

"I'd say you're a natural, honey, but since you brought it up, I wonder if you're still the adventurous kind."

Kay, still leaning over him, slowly kissed his full upper lip, then the bottom one, gently chewing on it. Releasing it, she said boldly, "I love adventure, you know that."

"Good. We're in the islands and we should take advantage of it, do you agree?"

"Yes." She didn't hesitate to answer. "But then it appears to me we are taking advantage of it." She dipped back to his mouth, to tease, to taste, to delight him.

"Hmm, yes, we are," he mumbled under the onslaught of her sweet mouth so expertly teasing his. "But I thought tomorrow, since we have the entire day free, we could get up early, catch a plane to Eleuthera and . . ."

"Wait, Sul." She lifted her head, pushing a heavy shock of hair behind an ear. "Eleuthera? Where is it? What is it?"

"Honey." He brought a hand up to a soft full breast and watched in rapt appreciation when his touch caused the soft little center to blossom into a tempting hard bud. "Eleuthera is one of the out islands. It's about seventy miles from here; it's tiny, more private. We'd be by ourselves; no chance of running into any of our group." His thumb began to lazily circle the pleasing little peak he'd helped to create.

"Oh, Sul, let's," Kay responded happily. "We can go over, spend all day and—"

"Hmm," he breathed, "let's make plans later." He moved his arm around her and pulled her closer. "Tomorrow can wait." His mouth took hers in an ardent kiss as he reversed their positions, turning her onto her back. Kay sighed and responded to him, arching her body up against him, loving the quickly heating lips moving on hers, the taste of the velvet tongue once more roaming her mouth. When finally the kiss ended and his lips slowly started moving down her body, Kay, rapidly releasing her hold on reality, let it go completely when Sullivan's mouth closed over her right nipple, tenderly drawing it into the warm, wet cavern of his mouth while his hands slid caressingly down her silky legs.

"Yes…tomorrow," she sighed and slid her hands into the rich dark hair of his head, pressing him closer to the full breast gleaming milky white beneath the face of the man bent to it.

Sullivan and Kay rose early the next morning. Kay, a pair of bright yellow slacks and a striped blouse covering a brief white bikini, sat close to Sullivan in the taxi that took them to the airport.

Sullivan, handsome and casual in a pair of snug-fitting white deck pants with a red and white pullover knit shirt

stretching across his muscular chest, had a pleased smile
playing at his full lips. A possessive arm around Kay's
shoulders, he reached for a cigarette. Kay took the matches,
lighting it for him.

"Sullivan," she said, holding the little flame up to the
filtered cigarette, "whatever happened to that gold lighter I
gave you?" She blew out the match and placed the packet
back inside his breast pocket.

Sullivan laughed and pulled her closer. "I'm ashamed to
tell you."

"You lost it."

"No, I broke it." Sullivan paused, shook his head and
admitted, "That first night you came back to town. You
know, when I was to meet you and the Shultses for dinner."

"Yes, you didn't come. You didn't want to see me."

"I did. I wanted to see you so badly that I ... Truth is I
threw the damned lighter across the room and the lid broke
off."

Kay showed no shock. She put an arm around his waist,
squeezed him and said, "Darling, I'd hoped you had
learned to control that temper of yours. Looks like I was
wrong."

Sullivan kissed the sweet, glowing face looking up at him.
"I'll try to do better. I thought I'd just about whipped it,
then you came back and, well, the lighter wasn't the only
thing that got thrown."

"Doesn't matter, I'll get you another lighter."

"No," he said softly, "I'll have the old one repaired. Do
it first thing when we get back to Denver."

Sullivan and Kay were hardly airborne before they were
once again descending. The little commuter plane glided to
a stop at Governor's Harbour Airport and Kay and Sullivan hurried for a taxi that took them up a very narrow road
to the ferry dock. Hopping on to the ferry, they were taken
to the Dunsmore town dock.

Kay, stepping from the ferry, cast her eyes to the tiny town on the small island. She felt Sullivan tugging on her hand, saying, "Let's go."

She fell into step, thinking he meant them to explore the old village with its neat two-and three-story buildings. He walked briskly and Kay hurried to keep up. He seemed to have a destination in mind.

They went directly to a quaint hotel where Sullivan let go of Kay's hand and strode directly to the desk. Kay let her eyes wander around the empty lobby, wondering idly if he intended for them to check in and spend the day in their room.

Soon he was walking back, taking her arm and smiling broadly. "I've made arrangements to have us ferried to a tiny, uninhabited island for a very private afternoon."

"You're teasing me," she arched her eyebrows.

"I'm not," he assured her. "The hotel dining room is going to pack us a lunch. We'll take the food, head back to the pier and meet our boat. Sound good?" He wore that relaxed, pleased-with-himself look she'd seen so many times and loved.

"Sounds wonderful," she said, thinking this was going to be one lovely Sunday.

And it was.

Less than an hour after leaving the Dunsmore town hotel, a wicker basket of food over Sullivan's bent arm, the pair stepped from the boat onto the hot, blindingly white sands of a minuscule island that belonged only to them for the day.

The smiling little man who'd transported them waved a cheerful goodbye, thus assuring the handsome couple of their privacy. He promised he'd return for them promptly at 8:00 p.m. In seconds he was only a speck on the emerald waters.

Sullivan stashed the food chest back off the beach, under dense, shading foliage, then turned and said, "Shall we take a swim before we eat?" His hands were already lifting to strip the red and white shirt up over his stomach and chest.

"Love to." Kay unzipped the bright yellow slacks, kicked off her thong sandals and stepped out of the pants.

Sullivan, speedier than Kay, stood stripped down to his white swim trunks. His dark eyes narrowed, intensely observing the lovely, slender woman shrugging out of a striped blouse. Kay, feeling those dark eyes on her, looked up, smiled nervously and tugged at the tight bikini bottom, jerking frantically at the high-riding fabric covering her buttocks.

"Are you forgetting?" Sullivan walked to her. "We're alone here. You don't have to tug on your suit. You don't even have to wear a suit."

"I'll wear a suit," she informed him and started for the water. He gave no reply, but he smiled devilishly. Kay felt a rush of blood to her face and had the feeling that before this lovely day ended, she'd be suitless and happy to be.

Together they played in the water, shouting, laughing, splashing, until they were out of breath and tired. Sullivan swung Kay up into his arms and carried her onto the beach, dumping her onto the big beach blanket spread close to the water's edge.

They lay on their backs in the sweltering sun, lazy, happy and soon hungry. Kay eagerly looked inside the big wicker hamper. "Sullivan," she said, "they've thought of everything. There's cold roast beef and ham and cheese and bread and wine and fruit."

They dozed for a time after their lunch, too full for activity. Kay stirred first, rolling easily to a sitting position. Beside her, Sullivan, resting on his stomach, dark cheek pressed against a bent forearm, slept peacefully.

Kay sighed with supreme happiness. They were here, alone, on this beautiful tiny island of their own. She hugged her knees thinking that surely all that life had to offer was present on this glorious, sun-drenched Sunday afternoon. Skies of cobalt blue held a few puffy white clouds high above. Sparkling crystals of sand, as white as the clouds, made a warm, cushioning bed for suntanned bodies. Water, so deep and clear she could see the bottom, rolled peacefully in to shore; the only sound, save the deep, even breathing of the handsome man asleep on his stomach.

Kay rose, stretched her arms over her head and walked across the hot sands to the cool water. She walked out until the emerald waves were slapping at her breasts, kicked off from the bottom and began to swim gracefully out, slicing through the clear water with swanlike strokes. Kay swam alone for a time, pausing now and again to push her hair from her eyes, treading water, paddling lazily with her arms and legs.

Kay, dunking her head over backward to sweep the long, wet tresses to the back of her head, gasped. Something was tugging on a toe. Kicking furiously, Kay quickly identified the pesky creature, laughing deep in her throat and purposely giving a broad brown back a stomp of her bare foot.

Sullivan surfaced in front of her. "How long have you been out here?" A long arm circled her waist.

"Not long. You were sleeping so deeply." She put her hands atop his wet gleaming shoulders.

"Hmm, well I'm wide awake now and ready for action." His eyes gleamed.

"Mister," she said cheerfully, "I'm afraid you've come to the wrong island for action."

"No," he countered, "the kind of action I'm seeking can only be found here." His hands were sliding up her rib cage to her breasts. Kay felt a shiver of excitement. His hand went back of her, deftly unhooked the skimpy top and pulled it away from her body while his eyes looked into hers. "Isn't that more comfortable?"

"Yes," she admitted, the white mounds of her naked breasts clearly visible in the crystal water.

"Then why not take off the rest?"

"Sul, do you really think . . . I mean what if . . ."

Ignoring her weak protests, Sullivan's hands were already sliding down over the gentle curve of her hips. One hand held the bikini top. Thumbs hooking into the briefs, he said, "I want us to swim together naked. Don't you want that, too, Kay?"

Kay could only nod. Never in her life had she skinny-dipped, and she was as eager as Sullivan to be completely naked in this beautiful clear water. Kay helped kick out of the wet suit, but looked at Sullivan with slightly frightened eyes when she saw his brown hand go high over his head as he tossed both pieces of her discarded garb onto the beach.

"I'll have to get out of the water without my—"

"Yes," he said, grinning wickedly. "You sure will."

Sullivan released her for a second, rid himself of his swim trunks, tossed them after Kay's suit and pulled her back into his arms. Despite the coldness of the water, heat emanated from the two eager bodies pressing naked together as Sullivan drew Kay's slender legs around his waist and kissed her long and lovingly.

"That's all you get for now," he teased her. "Don't want you getting spoiled."

Kay playfully nipped at a gleaming wet shoulder, pushed him away and swam out toward the green and blue of the horizon, fleetingly deciding that swimsuits should be outlawed. The best and easiest way for a body to slash through the water was quite naturally *sans* clothing of any kind.

Sullivan swam out to her, turned over and backstroked very gracefully along beside her. They swam, they raced, they floated, they had a water fight. They walked naked out of the surf and Kay felt not the slightest twinge of embarrassment. Wasn't this the way it should be?

They stretched out on their rumpled blanket to rest, lying on their backs, eyes closed against the direct rays of the sun. The water rapidly dried on their bare bodies, and Kay let her hair spread out around her, too lazy to run a comb through it.

She was almost dozing when he said very softly, his breath a warm whisper upon her cheek, "Kay, I love you."

Kay's eyes slid open just as his mouth came down on hers, warm and gentle. For a sweet, languid time Sullivan's lips feathered kisses over her hot face, always returning to her mouth. The kisses grew longer, hotter, sweeter as his mouth ground into hers, making her long for and need what she knew was going to happen here on this hot, sandy beach.

Sullivan's mouth left hers and went to her soft shoulders. His long, bare body nestled closer to hers and Kay felt her passions rising rapidly. The movements of his mouth upon her skin made her squirm and sigh and murmur his name. Slowly, surely that male mouth was moving down, his tongue gently pressing into the hollow of her throat, then continuing to kiss a wet, warm path to a quivering, anxious breast.

When he reached the crest, Sullivan raised his head for just one instant, admiring with his heated gaze her lush, shimmering breasts with their shy pink peaks pointed toward the sun.

"Sweet," he murmured, bent his head and took a nipple into his mouth. Gently he sucked, leisurely loving her, pleasuring her, until Kay's eyes were opening and closing with ecstasy and her hands were twisting in his thick, damp hair. Sullivan groaned as he sucked at the hard little peaks until Kay thought she could surely stand the sweet agony no longer.

His mouth slid lower still, kissing a path down her middle, pausing at her flat, sun-warmed stomach. His mouth slid lower and he kissed her. Kay's shocked eyes flew open when his tongue began to stroke silky, sensitive flesh. She began to squirm, trying to pull free, but Sullivan's hands clung to her hips to hold her to him and his masterful mouth soon had Kay writhing in sweet, undreamed-of torture.

She no longer tried to pull free. Nearer and nearer to the brink Sullivan took her, pulling back just before total fulfillment, pressing soothing, soft caresses to her shimmering thighs until Kay, calming a little, would gasp as that heated mouth again closed over the silken fire to lick and love and drive her higher and higher. When at last total joy burst within her, Kay screamed out in ecstasy and frantically bucked and writhed against him.

Sullivan stayed with her, his hands grasping the naked smooth flesh of her bottom, holding her to him, letting the jerking of her little body subside and finally pass. Only then did his mouth leave her.

She lay limp and listless upon the sand, at peace with the world and herself and her man. Too tired to move, too happy to speak, Kay let Sullivan gently enfold her spent body, pressing it tenderly to his, his lips upon her hair, her face resting on his chest. Beneath her ear, his heartbeat, strong and rapid, told her he was still in an extremely excited state, as did the swollen, heated maleness jerking against her thigh.

Sullivan, the blood pounding in his ears, heat engulfing his body, gratefully eased her onto her back, moved over her, murmured, "I wish I could wait for a while, but I..." A look of torture flashed in his dark, expressive eyes as he entered her, moaning with pleasure.

Slowly he moved within her and to Kay's complete surprise, she soon began to come alive once again, to enjoy, to feel her body heating, to crave and anticipate an encore of release. Sullivan sensed it, slowed his movements, eager to take her with him to total bliss. Exquisitely he loved her.

Kay responded to his expertise and soon was moving erotically with him, whispering his name, nibbling at his shoulder, feeling that sweet knot of fire building, building until the roaring inferno had to be quenched. The explosion came for them both and they moaned and sighed, tossed and buffeted by a force greater than them.

Slowly the waves of rapture subsided. They lay there on the sand, two sated, happy lovers, naked in paradise, free of clothing or guilt or cares.

Save a jet trail high overhead, there were no reminders of civilization here in their private paradise. The slap of the waves upon the shore was the only sound.

Sullivan finally spoke. "How do you like your adventure?"

Kay's answer was a shy smile, a soft kiss and a hug so tight Sullivan could feel it gripping his happy heart.

Nine

_____

Are you sorry we're leaving paradise?" Sullivan's voice made Kay turn from the plane's window to smile warmly at him.

Tightening her slender fingers on the long brown ones laced through them, she leaned near his ear and confided, "We're not leaving it, Sul. Heaven is where you are."

Sullivan's dark head turned to hers. His gaze dropped to the soft, parted lips only inches from his own. He swallowed hard. "Damn, I'd like to kiss you," he said honestly. "Don't look at me like that, honey."

"Sorry." She giggled happily. "I know what you mean. It's been how long since last we kissed? An hour?"

"Longer." He nodded decisively. "I'm not sure I can take it much longer."

Kay felt her stomach fluttering. "You'll have to. It would never do for the Q102 morning-show team to toss all decorum to the winds and start kissing on an airliner in front of a planeload of loyal listeners."

"You're right," he conceded, tipping his wrist up to look at his watch. "We land back in Denver at noon. Jeff will be there to meet us. With any luck, we can be at my place by one o'clock."

Kay shook her head. "Yes, but you know Jeff. He'll insist we join him for lunch so he can hear all about—"

"He can feed himself. What I hunger for is you."

Kay's eyes darted around as high color rose in her face. "Sh," she cautioned. "Suppose someone should hear you."

Sullivan laughed, crooked a long finger for her to lean closer. Kay cast one more nervous glance at the passengers seated across from them and leaned to him. Sullivan's lips brushed her hair and his breath was warm against her ear. Very softly he whispered to her, his voice so low she had to strain to hear. Kay listened intently. Her already flushed face grew crimson and she drew away from him, her blue eyes huge.

Sullivan observed her with a wide, teasing grin. "Kay," he drawled easily, "you're cute when you're embarrassed."

Kay snatched her hand from his and said indignantly, "Sullivan Ward, I am not embarrassed!"

"Good," he teased, "I've got some more ideas for—"

"Hush, and I mean it," she snapped, her blue eyes flashing fire.

"All right," he said, good-naturedly, the mischief fleeing his dark eyes. "Love me?"

Kay sighed, leaned her head back against the tall seat and nodded. "I do," she breathed. "Oh, I do."

Jeff Kerns stood at the airport gate waiting. His eyes twinkled when he saw Kay coming toward him, smiling. Sullivan was right behind her. He, too, was smiling. It was a brand of smile Jeff had not seen on Sullivan Ward's face in years.

"So it's Adam and Eve with their clothes back on." Jeff stepped forward to greet them and saw the quick flash of shame on Kay's pretty face while Sullivan shot him a silencing look from over her head. "My little attempt at humor." Jeff directed his speech to Kay. "I mean you've been down to Paradise Island, you see, and so—"

"Ever considered a simple greeting, like 'Hello, glad you're back'?" Sullivan asked, his arm going possessively around the blushing Kay to pull her to his side.

Jeff shoved the navy watch cap he wore a little nearer to his eyebrows. Grinning knowingly, he lifted his shoulders. "Hello. Glad you're back."

Kay, relaxing, laughed, reached out a small hand, slid her fingers up the lapel of Jeff's heavy wool jacket and pulled his face close to hers. She gave his jaw a peck and whispered, "Does it show that much, Jeff?"

Jeff laughed, cast a glance up at Sullivan's dark face, saw that he, too, was smiling easily and said, "Honey, my old-maid aunt could see through you two. You might as well have rubber-stamped your foreheads."

Too much in love to care that he was wise to their changed relationship, Kay said, "You're probably right, Jeff, but on the off chance that it's not all that evident to the rest of the world, think you could keep it to yourself?"

"Me?" He jammed a thumb into his chest, his blue eyes wide and innocent. "Do I look like the kind of guy who'd go around—"

"Jeffrey," Sullivan interrupted, "let's see to the bags; we're tired and we want to get home."

"Too bad, buddy," Jeff informed him. "The gang's waiting at Leo's and I told them you'd be there."

"I don't care what you told them, we are not going."

"Now, Sul," Kay gently interrupted, "it's sweet of them to want to see us. We can hardly let them down."

Sullivan made a face. "But we . . ."

"Come on, man," Jeff scolded. "They want to buy your lunch. It would be rude if you didn't show up."

Sullivan glared at Jeff. "Rude? Who are you to tell me about rudeness?"

"Sul." Kay's voice was no more than a whisper.

"Yeah, honey?" She had Sullivan's undivided attention.

"I think we should join them."

"All right."

Jeff Kerns laughed at Sullivan's hasty acquiescence, but Sullivan was much too happy a man to care.

The whole crew, including Sam Shults, did indeed await them at Leo's place, warmly welcoming the pair back to Denver where the frozen ground was still covered with snow from the heavy storm of a week earlier. Sullivan, shaking hands with all his jocks, never released his hold on Kay.

Kay felt a thrill of pleasure from his easy display of affection. Sullivan, his eyes warming each time they rested on her, chatted easily with everyone there. All the while, Kay felt loved and cherished and gloriously happy.

Her toes curled inside her shoes when Sullivan, heatedly debating the chances of K105 radio, Q102's biggest competitor picked up one of her hands from the white tablecloth, raised it to his lips and pressed warm, loving kisses to her fingertips while he spoke.

"How can you sit there and tell me you think their afternoon drive man can touch Jeff?" His question was directed at Dale Kitrell. "Eight to five says Jeff will beat him by at least five share points."

"Oh, man, you're not listening." Dale Kitrell reached for a pretzel. "That's not what I meant. Their afternoon man can't beat Jeff, I know that."

"Please, fellas." Jeff raised his voice to a falsetto and wrung his hands. "Don't fight over me."

Ignoring Jeff, Sullivan said, "Then what, Dale?" He lowered Kay's hand slowly from his lips, studying it as though he'd never seen it before. Tenderly he wrapped her fingers around his biceps, his hand resting atop hers. "You think—"

"I think their numbers will be better than their last book, Ward. Their new program director is a talented guy."

Kay barely listened. She was tired and content. She let the men argue and discuss the upcoming ratings; they were the furthest thing from her mind at the moment. She listened to the deep, pleasing timbre of Sullivan's voice and silently planned for the evening before them. Tingles of expecta-

ion causing her to smile, Kay looked up and saw Janelle
Davis's eyes on her.

Janelle smiled immediately and quietly nodded to Kay.
Kay's face broke into a wide, happy grin. She had the other
woman's approval. Janelle knew what had happened and
he was giving her blessing to the pair. Kay was glad.
Somehow it mattered very much to her to have Janelle's
sanction. Kay's fingers tightened on the muscular arm she
held and she nodded her head to Janelle, communicating to
the kind and gentle woman that she was deeply in love with
Sullivan Ward and would never again hurt him.

Janelle read the message and seemed satisfied.

When Kay caught herself wondering if the laughing,
friendly gang around the table would ever break up, Jeff
rose, pulled his cap onto his head and announced, "It's late
but if you guys will all stay right where you are, I have to run
across the street to the station and do my show but I'll be
back just as soon as it ends."

Everyone laughed. Sullivan seized the opportunity to say,
"Kay and I have to go, too." He pushed back his chair, cut
his eyes to her and added, "We need some rest." He was
rising, reaching for her coat.

"Sullivan." Janelle opened her handbag, bringing out a
set of keys. "The Mercedes is parked in the underground lot
of the building."

Sullivan took his keys. "Thanks, Janelle. Appreciate it."
His eyes swept around the table. "See you all tomorrow."

"Yes," Kay echoed. "And thanks for this welcome home;
it was fun."

Sullivan and Kay crossed the street with Jeff, said goodbye and took the elevator to the underground garage. Sullivan transferred their luggage from Jeff's van to his
Mercedes, crawled behind the wheel, winked at Kay, patted
her knee and said, "Your place or mine?"

Kay laughed, slid over to him and said, "I hate decisions."

Sullivan smiled at her, took her left hand and placed it o
his sinewy thigh. "Then for the rest of this day, you'll no
have to make any."

Kay sighed, spread her fingers on the hard, male limb
feeling the pull of the muscles beneath the fabric of his pant
as he pressed his foot down onto the gas pedal, easing th
powerful car out of the covered garage and onto the bus
streets. They said nothing driving to Sullivan's apartment
They listened to Jeff's afternoon show on the car radio
laughing uproariously over almost everything he said. Eve
as they did, both knew that the laughter was much, mucl
more than appreciation of the wit of their old friend.

They were happy lovers. The world, cold and froze
though it was in Denver, was incredibly beautiful. Life wa
sweet. Everything was funny. Sullivan and Kay were sti
laughing when they stood outside Sullivan's front door, Ka
jiggling the key in the lock, Sullivan standing behind her
loaded down with luggage.

Once inside, the laughter subsided and finally ceased.

Sullivan dropped the suitcases to the floor, drew off hi
gloves and hurried to build a fire in the grate. Kay, leavin
on her coat, found the thermostat and shoved it up to eighty
degrees. She stood shivering before the tall glass windows
watching Sullivan pile piñon logs atop one another. Soor
flames shot high into the air and Sullivan came over to Kay.

Rubbing his hands up and down her arms, he said solic-
itously, "Cold, sweet baby?"

"Hmm." She nodded. "Freezing."

Sullivan pulled her close, lifted a hand to her chin and
tipped her face up to his. "Think I can warm your blood?"

Kay tilted her head. "Like to try?"

Sullivan grinned, slowly pulled her coat apart, slipped his
hands inside and lowered his mouth to hers. "Yes," he said,
his voice low and husky, "I want to warm you. To build a
fire inside you."

His lips touched hers in a slow, unhurried kiss. Inside the
coat, his hands went to her sweatered back and he gently
urged her body against his. Kay's hands hung loosely at her
sides as she let Sullivan take complete charge. She let him

hold the soft contours of her body to his solid length. She
let his mouth move leisurely upon her lips, warming, awak-
ning, persuading.

It was glorious.

Like clay in the hands of a master sculptor, Kay was his
to touch and smooth and mold into his own creation. He did
just that, expertly changing the shivering woman into a
heated, naked work of art.

The transformation was done with love and patience by
the artist. When his masterpiece was stretched bare and
beautiful before him in front of the roaring fire, Sullivan
disrobed and made love to the lovely, living creation. Indeed, he became a part of the priceless art object.

Sullivan and Kay were back on their early-morning radio
show the very next day. Working together had always been
challenging and fun. Now there was an added dimension to
their relationship and the dim control room fairly crackled
with electricity on that cold, dark morning.

There was an abundance of touching and playful kissing
between the pair as records spun and cassettes unwound.
When they weren't kissing, they were laughing. Everything
seemed outrageously comical as their spirits soared. Love
had conquered and its warm glow made the cold winter day
appear brighter, the music prettier, the coffee more palat-
able, their well-timed patter more humorous.

A lengthy record played on the turntable. Kay, her chair
turned to Sullivan's, leaned forward to say, "When do you
look for the rating book?" Kay was looking into his eyes
and saw a puzzling flicker in their dark depths. It immediately vanished and Sullivan smiled.

"Be any day now, Kay."

"You're surely not worried about it, are you?"

"No." His answer was a little short, the tone of voice a bit
brusque.

"Sullivan," she questioned, her eyes narrowed, "is
something wrong? I thought you were very optimistic about
our expected ratings. Why the—"

"Sweetheart." He smiled, lifted a hand up to cup a cheek "I am positive that our show will get a very high rating There's no doubt in my mind."

"Then I don't understand." She studied his face. "When I brought it up you—I don't know—" she lifted her slende shoulders "—you looked worried."

"Darling," Sullivan laughed easily and leaned closer "You're imagining things, I assure you. Now give me a hug before this song ends."

Relaxing completely, Kay smiled, threw her arms around his neck and pressed her cheek to his, supremely happy. She never saw the look of doubt filling the expressive black eyes of the man she loved.

Sullivan clasped her to him and silently battled the small tight core of fear expanding in his abdomen. He was sure they'd get a good book. Positive. And that entire broadcasting industry would know of their success.

Would he lose her again?

Sullivan bit his bottom lip, closed his eyes and tightened his embrace.

That very morning, during the nine o'clock news break, an out-of-breath, excited Jeff Kerns, hurried into the control room. Sam Shults was right behind him, grinning from ear to ear.

The familiar blue and white Arbitron rating book was clutched in the blunt fingers of Sam's beefy right hand. Sullivan saw it first.

Sam lifted it high, shook it at them and announced, "It's here, kids. Just came in."

Kay swallowed and grabbed Sullivan's hand. His dark, smooth face was devoid of expression, but she saw a muscle dance in his lean jaw and his fingers gave hers a brief squeeze. Evenly, he said, "Out with it, Sammy. Are we the hottest team in radio or not?" An easy smile lifted the corners of his full mouth.

"Sullivan, Kay—" Sam Shults, looking from one to the other, proudly confirmed "—it's even better than we'd hoped for! I mean your morning show pulled a whopping sixteen share...more than our wildest expectations. Congratulations to you both. You two are an unequaled hit. No one else came close.''

He leaned over the control panel to shake Sullivan's hand. He handed the rating book to Sullivan, gave the beaming Kay a kiss on the cheek and said, ''The champagne will be cooling in my office. Come on in as soon as your show ends.'' The stocky man turned and went to the door. Pausing there, he turned and said, ''I'm just delighted, kids. About the fantastic ratings and about everything else. You know what I mean.'' Sam's face pinkened.

''No, we don't know, what else?'' Jeff was his usual devilish self. ''What are you trying to say, boss?''

Sam Shults shook his head, made a dismissive gesture in Jeff's direction and left the room.

''So.'' Jeff turned his full attention to Sullivan and Kay. ''How about that book?'' Sullivan was already back in his chair, bent over the columns of figures denoting audience shares. ''I even came up one percent. But best of all, K105 took the gas. I mean we sucked 'em right up our tail pipe in every time slot. You guys must have taken nearly all of their previous audience.''

Sullivan continued to study the book before him. Kay, her eyes alight with happiness, leaned over his shoulder, following the movement of the dark thumb hurriedly sliding down the columns of telling numbers. ''Did we, Sul? Did we take our biggest competitor's listening audience?'' The sound of her tinkling, happy laughter filled the control room.

''Sure did, honey.'' Sullivan never looked up. ''You stole 'em all.''

''No, Sul, *we* stole them.''

Sullivan's dark eyes lifted from the book. ''You're sweet, but in last spring's rating book I didn't—''

''Damn you, Sullivan,'' Jeff cut in, while Kay looked worriedly at Sullivan's hard, handsome face. ''Man, you're crying with a loaf of bread under each arm. What the hell would it take to make you happy?'' Jeff shook his head and added, "I'm going to get a head start on the champagne. See you guys later."

After Jeff had gone, Kay said, "Sullivan Ward, you just listen to me. We, and I repeat we, are a success. Not me. Not you. Us. The two of us together are a hit. We're a team and it's the team that pulled high ratings."

Sullivan lifted his eyes to hers. Kay smiled, her lips parted her eyes pleading with him. Sullivan felt his chest expand with love for this beautiful woman who was every bit as sweet as she was lovely. He smiled, lifted a hand up to slide his fingers into her hair at the side of her head and said in a deep, sure voice, "Kiss me, partner."

Kay's smile grew brilliant. "I will," she breathed, slowly leaning to him. "And it takes us both to do that, too. Teamwork. Your mouth and mine."

Sullivan chuckled and the sound of his deep laughter rumbling from his chest filled Kay with added happiness. Her lips touched his. Laughter ceased, but dark eyes, wide open, looked into hers as his mouth took command, kissing her with fiery abandon. Kay did her part, too. After all, it was a team effort; a feat impossible to perform alone.

Ten

The week following the arrival of the fantastic rating book was one of sweet, undiluted pleasure for everyone's favorite radio team. Kay and Sullivan were together every moment, day and night, happily learning all the little idiosyncrasies of each other's complex personalities.

Kay learned that Sullivan Ward always put on his socks and shoes before stepping into his pants. She thought it odd and extremely funny. She'd go into peals of happy laughter when the man she loved stood before the mirror brushing his hair, dressed in shirt, shoes and socks, his long legs bare.

She found that the very last thing he did before going to sleep was to comb his hair, a habit she found endearingly charming. The first thing he did on waking was to reach, bleary-eyed, for his first cigarette of the day. He liked black coffee, toast and three scrambled eggs for breakfast. Kay, sipping freshly squeezed fruit juice, watched him and wondered how anyone could eat anything at 4:30 a.m.

Kay learned that Sullivan Ward liked to lie on his long sofa in the evenings, with her stretched out beside him while he flipped from one channel to the next on the television, read a book, and talked to her all at the same time, remarkably following the plotline of the show they watched, comprehending the book he was reading, and never missing one word she said to him. He was a strange, complex, totally fascinating person, this man she loved so dearly. She looked forward to all the happy months and years it would take to fully understand him.

Sullivan, too, found there were many things he'd never known about the charmer now sharing his apartment. She was a sweet, talkative companion, but she said nothing for at least forty-five minutes after awakening each morning. He found this strange, since the moment he opened his eyes, he was awake and ready to discuss the day's plans. It took only a couple of mornings for him to learn that Kay liked being kissed awake, but conversation was taboo. He didn't mind. She was so irresistibly cute and warm when she woke up; silvery hair all tousled, her sweet, soft lips moving under his. What did it matter that she frowned if he asked her a question?

Sullivan also learned that he'd never fully realized just how lonely his life had been without this woman whose tinkling laughter was music to his ears. She came to his arms whenever he held them out to her, which was often, dropping whatever she happened to be doing to step into his embrace. She was his sweet, adorable Kay; his to touch and teach and treasure.

That's how it would always be.

Sullivan and Kay were well aware that the unprecedented success of their morning show made their services infinitely more valuable. They'd discussed at length the amount of increase they planned to request at contract time.

Rating points of the magnitude they'd pulled meant much more expensive commercial spots in their morning show, which led to an increase of hundreds of thousands of dollars in revenue for Q102. Since they were responsible for the value of the thirty- and sixty-second commercials shooting skyward, they were entitled to be momentarily rewarded and were well aware of it. So was Sam Shults. He'd already hinted at a figure he had in mind. Sullivan had smiled easily, knowing Sam Shults would offer far less than the amount he was authorized by ownership. Bargaining was all a part of the game. Sullivan Ward was good at it.

Sullivan and Kay, their air trick finished for the day, were seated in Sullivan's corner office, Sullivan again going over with Kay what he thought they should ask for in the way of their salary increases. Kay, in her hand an envelope of photographs she'd taken on their Bahamas trip with the tiny gold camera Sullivan had given her, was nodding her agreement while she studied the pictures before her.

"Oh, Sul—" she looked up, interrupting him "—you've got to see this one." She handed the picture across his desk. It was one she'd taken of him standing beside the plane, just before they departed from Miami to return to Denver. "You look like some handsome, famous movie star." She smiled at him.

Sullivan glanced at the picture, handed it back and said, "Show me the ones I took of you."

Kay complied and watched as his dark eyes lit up. He held a small picture between thumb and forefinger, smiling broadly. The photo showed only Kay's face and bare shoulders; she was frowning into the camera and in her eyes was a distinct look of embarrassment.

"I love this, honey." He grinned at her. "I want this for my wallet."

Kay shook her head. "If you ever..."

"...tell anyone that you were naked when I snapped this and that's why you're scowling?" His hooded eyes mocked her. "I won't, sweetheart, but I know, that makes the picture precious to me."

Kay shrugged. "You're weird, you know that, Sullivan?"

"Yeah, but when I look at this picture I can see your..." The buzzing of the intercom on the corner of his desk interrupted them. Sullivan grimaced and punched in the button. "What?"

Sherry Jones's excited voice filled his ear. "Sullivan, is Kay in there with you?"

"Yes, she is."

"Oh, good. Tell her that she has a very important telephone call from ABC." Sherry drew in a quick breath. "That's in New York City, Sullivan, did you know that?"

"Yes," he said, "I knew that. I'll tell her."

"All right, the caller's on line three. Tell Kay it's urgent."

Sullivan replaced the receiver. "I suppose you heard that, Kay. You've a call on line three."

"Hand me the phone, will you."

"You might want to take it in your office, Kay."

Kay rose from the chair, smiling. "Why on earth would I want to do that? I've no secrets from you." She leaned over, punched in the blinking light, lifted the phone and said, "This is Kay Clark."

Sullivan, lounging nonchalantly back in his chair, hands laced behind his head, watched Kay. He saw her eyes widen and sparkle with excitement, and his stomach tightened. Nervously she twisted a long strand of hair while she nodded and said, "Yes, yes. I . . . well, thank you." She listened for several minutes, then was again speaking, her voice animated, a look of shocked elation glowing in her eyes.

Sullivan never changed his lazy position. He looked for all the world like a man totally at ease, in charge, relaxed. Sullivan's reaction was a great shock to Kay when, after she'd ended her telephone conversation she honestly informed him that it had been the program director from ABC in New York City. He was telling her that they'd seen the ratings and wondered if she'd be at all interested in flying up to discuss the possibility of becoming the first air partner of their dynamic morning-show star.

Sullivan's hands slowly came from behind his head. His jaw clenched and his eyes were cold and hard when he said, "So when do you leave?"

Kay looked at him and laughed. "Leave? Sul, I didn't say—"

Rage, unchecked, showed on his face and his voice took on a deadly timbre. "Your eyes said it for you." He rose from his chair, shoved his hands into his pockets and walked to the window.

Kay felt terror rise to her throat. Those eyes looked so furious, so menacing. She knew she must at once clear up any misunderstanding on his part or she was in danger of losing him again. Kay hurried to him, put a hand on his shoulder and said softly, "Listen, I don't—"

Sullivan spun around to face her. "Listen? I did, Kay. I heard every word you said and I don't remember a single no coming from those lovely little lips."

Kay's apprehension grew alarmingly. "Sullivan, you didn't hear me say yes, either. My lord, give me a little credit."

"Credit?" he parroted. "Oh, sweetheart, you get all the credit. You're the smoothest little number on the airwaves." His black eyes snapped with fury. "New York City!" He shook his dark head. "Just what you wanted. That's wonderful, Kay, truly great."

"I've no intention of going, Sul, I just—"

"Why in hell not?" he barked. "That's what you've been waiting for, isn't it?"

"No, it's not." She was losing her temper fast. "You know very well it's not."

"I know you told me New York City is where you belong."

"I said that only because... because you made me."

"Damn it, I didn't make you say anything, or do anything." He was leaning close, glaring down at her. "When are you ever going to take responsibility for your actions?"

"The same could be said for you, Sullivan." Kay gritted her teeth, balled her hands into tight fists and tried to regain control. "Sullivan, don't let this happen. Don't let this happen to..."

"There you go again," he interrupted angrily. "What have I let happen? Answer me that, will you? Let you use my phone to talk to your next partner? That it?"

"I can't believe you, Sullivan." She shook her head to clear it.

"Well, then, sweetheart, I'm ahead of you on that score, because I sure as hell can believe you." He laughed hollowly. "Yes, baby, it's all too easy for me to believe you. And if you think for one minute I'm blaming you, set your mind at ease." Sullivan turned to walk away.

Kay, her fists immediately coming unclenched, grabbed frantically at his arm. "No! Don't walk away from me. Damn you, Sullivan. I'm not going to let you." Her face was flushing with heat, her hands trembling with emotion. "You stand here and face me and tell me that you want me to stay here with you!"

"No way, sweetheart." Sullivan sneered down at her. "I'm not about to give you that final satisfaction."

"Satisfaction?" She stared at him incredulously. "You're not making a great deal of sense. The satisfaction I want is for you to tell me, and mean it, that you can't bear to have me leave you; that you want me."

High color stained Sullivan's face as he said heatedly, "I'm not going to do it!"

"Why not?" Kay was shouting now, feeling the volcanic situation slipping out of control. "Please, Sul, please." Tears were threatening and her voice broke. "Must you always be so stubborn and blind?"

"You're the one who's blind, Kay. Blind to yourself." His voice was calmer now, sadder. "I wish you could have seen the look in your eyes when you were speaking on the phone. That look said a lot, Kay. Too much for me to ignore."

"No." Kay tried desperately to make him understand. "It's not the way you think." She clung to his arm, frantically pleading her case. "Darling, of course I was excited that the top station called wanting me. I can't deny that; it's very flattering and I was thrilled, I'll admit it, but—"

"Kay, I understand, really I do. Who wouldn't be thrilled to get an offer from one of the top radio stations in the country?" He was speaking now in low, modulated tones, the color leaving his face, his coolness returning, and for some reason that terrified Kay more than had he remained furious. "Dear, it's the chance of a lifetime. I'm pleased for you." Sullivan smiled.

Heart thumping against her ribs, Kay felt dizzy, ill. "Sul." She sighed. "Don't—oh, dear God, Sullivan, tell me to stay. Say you can't let me go."

For what seemed an eternity, his eyes impaled her and Kay held her breath, praying to hear the words she was straining to hear with every fiber of her being. The silence was deafening. They stood facing each other, their world teetering on the brink of destruction.

Finally Sullivan sighed. "Kay, I am not going to tell you to stay."

Kay released her breath. Pride, hurt and her own stubborn will mixed to make her say resolutely, "Very well, Sullivan, don't." She tried bravely to smile though her bottom lip trembled with her effort. "I can't make you, but I'll tell you one thing." She gulped for a breath. "This time it really is your fault. If your arrogance and pride are so great that you can't bring yourself to ask me to stay here with you, then we both lose, darling, because I will leave. I'll go to New York City and I'll do the best job I possibly can and in time I'll forget about you." Kay paused, reached out, put a hand to Sullivan's downcast face, making him look at her once again. "It is my second choice, Sullivan. Do you hear me? Don't ever forget that."

Kay looked up at him, studying the depths of his dark eyes. She saw there an unmistakable sorrow. It touched her, but not enough to keep her from dropping her hand from his face, turning, stepping past him and walking determinedly to his office door.

The door closed behind her and Sullivan stood rigid where she'd left him. He couldn't believe it had happened again.

Kay went into her small office at the opposite end of the hall, slammed the door behind her and leaned back against it. Pulses pounding in her ears, knees suddenly too watery to support her, she hurried to her chair, dropping down into it before the threatening dimness could overcome her.

Kay leaned back and closed her eyes. Behind her eyelids she still saw Sullivan standing there looking at her, mute, refusing to ask her to stay.

Kay's eyes opened. She was overcome with a case of violent trembling and felt for a moment that she might be ill. She sat there, shaking, and throughout she kept hoping that any moment the closed door to her office would fly open and Sullivan Ward would storm in, saying he was sorry, that he didn't mean it, that he couldn't stand to lose her.

It didn't happen.

An hour passed. An hour of agony, regret, disappointment and finally acceptance. Kay's trembling had ceased. The pounding of her heart had slowed to a steady rhythmic pace. Muscles had lost their tenseness. A great weariness now claimed her.

Kay pushed back her chair, took her handbag from the bottom drawer of her desk and left the station, ignoring the questioning, lifted auburn eyebrows of Sherry Jones at the reception desk.

"Kay—" the young woman shot out of her chair "—this is the first time I've seen you without Sullivan since—I mean, where are you going? Is something wrong? Will you be back after—"

Kay gave her a forced smile. "Sherry, I'm going home and I won't be back today."

"Well, sure. Kay, if someone calls shall I tell them that you went home?"

"Just take a message, Sherry. I'll see you tomorrow."

"Okay, but Kay?"

Kay sighed. "Yes?"

"Well, I'm just dying to know about, you know, New York. I couldn't believe it when they told me it was ABC calling, I just about had a . . . what did they want?"

"They want me to come to New York to discuss a position there."

Hazel eyes widened. "Oh, Kay!" Sherry shrieked. "That's just wonderful, but of course you told them you weren't interested."

"Sherry, I told them nothing of the kind." Kay smiled and started to move past the young girl's desk.

Sherry's hand went to her hips. "Kay Clark," she said in a voice loud enough that a couple of salesmen looked up from their desks in the adjoining room. "You surely wouldn't consider leaving Sullivan!"

Kay, biting her bottom lip, simply shook her head and hurried out the double doors without answering.

The winter sun was setting and Kay, alone in her apartment, thought idly how soon something becomes a habit. It was strange to be alone in this place she'd thought of as home until a week ago. She'd not stayed a night here since the eve of the Bahamas trip.

Since she and Sullivan had returned from that glorious holiday, she'd spent every night with him in his penthouse apartment across town. In exactly one week's time it had become very natural to take all her showers in his brown-tiled bath, to eat her meals from his chrome-and-glass table, to sleep like an infant in his big bed, a pair of strong, protective arms holding her close through the cold winter nights.

Kay sighed and rose from her couch. Listlessly she sauntered into her spotless kitchen, opened the refrigerator door and peered disinterestedly inside. She saw nothing there but a couple of colas, a bottle of catsup and a stick of margarine. Nothing at all to eat. It mattered little; she was not very hungry.

Kay closed the door. She'd restock tomorrow. There was no hurry. She could open a can of soup later if she got hungry. She shoved her hands into the back pockets of her jeans and padded back into the living room.

The last rays of the dying sun had just slipped below the Front Range. It was a beautiful sight. Shades of pink and purple streaked the sky, a pretty pastel backdrop for the majestic mountains framed in the soft, fading light.

She'd learned this past week that sunset was Sullivan's favorite time of day. He'd insisted, about this time every evening, that all lights in his apartment be switched off and that the two of them, their arms wrapped around each other, stretch out on the plush carpet before the two-story glass in his den to watch the spectacular magic light display. They'd lain there together, he pointing out all the vivid hues and changing colors until all the lovely light had disappeared and the Rockies were no longer visible against the sky.

Kay's hands came out of her pockets. Slowly she sank to her knees before the glass, her eyes riveted to the western horizon. A knifing pain shot through her heart and Kay sat back on her bare heels, lifted her hands to cover her face and cried. Her shoulders shook with her sobs. It felt very good to weep. Kay gave in to it, crying her heart out while the last light left the sky. When the tears ceased falling, darkness had crept into the room, matching the sad young woman's mood.

Throughout the long, lonely evening, Kay couldn't keep from hoping that the phone would ring, that it would be Sullivan saying he was sorry, that he wanted to come over. She was still hoping for a phone call when she crawled tiredly into her bed at midnight.

It was cold in her bed. So cold. Kay assumed the fetal position and longed for the arms that had held her only the night before.

Sullivan was coolly congenial when Kay walked into the control room the next morning. Treating each other like polite strangers, they said little, their conversation sporadic until he swung their mikes into position and the morning show was underway. The show, like always, was professional and polished. They laughed and chatted, easily convincing their listening audience that they were in high spirits and having loads of fun.

At ten o'clock, Sullivan led them into the news, flipped off the mikes and rose. He exited the control room without a word to Kay.

Kay remained for a moment in her chair. When she stood up, she'd made up her mind. Nodding absently to Ace Black, who'd just come in to do his midday trick, Kay went directly to her office and called New York. That done, she

ose, took a deep breath and walked with cool determina-
ion down the long corridor to Sullivan's office.

She knocked on his door and stepped inside as soon as he
alled out. "Sullivan," she said immediately, "I need a
ouple of days off from work." His dark, penetrating eyes
lowly lifted from the papers spread out on his desk. Kay
net his gaze. "For personal reasons, I need to miss work on
Monday and Tuesday mornings." She stood looking at him,
er hands clasped in front of her, waiting for him to ask her
why she needed the time off.

"Sure, Kay." He surprised her. "I see no problem."

"Sullivan, the reason I want—"

"You need not explain," he said dismissively. "You
aven't missed a day. You're entitled." The eyes lowered
ack to the papers on his desk.

"Thank you," Kay said, cleared her throat needlessly and
dded, "Ah, Sullivan, I was wondering if I could come by
our place this evening and—and pick up my things."

"By all means," he answered without raising his head.

Kay told herself she had to be the world's biggest fool, or
t least the world's biggest optimist, as she painstakingly
ressed that night to go to Sullivan's apartment. She'd called
nd gotten his permission to come by around seven to col-
ect her personal items.

Now, while she brushed her long, shiny, freshly sham-
ooed hair, Kay felt tingles of excitement and hope. Per-
aps when she arrived and they were once again alone inside
is apartment, he'd weaken and ask her to stay. She'd fling
erself right into his arms and breathlessly proclaim she'd
ever be out of his sight again.

Kay, wanting to appear casual yet appealing, appraised
he soft, clinging sweater of pale blue, its low neckline re-
ealing smooth creamy flesh. A small gold coin on a deli-
ate link chain rested in the valley of her breasts. Her tight
esigner jeans hugged her rounded hips and small waist.
Kay grabbed a gray wool jacket and hurried down to her
Porsche, heart beginning to speed pleasantly.

Half an hour later she stood outside Sullivan's door. When she'd rung his buzzer downstairs in the outer lobby, he'd answered promptly, as though he might be as eager as she. Anticipation rising, Kay was smiling when Sullivan flung open his heavy front door.

The smile froze on her face.

"Hi," he said evenly, looking down on her from lazy-lidded eyes. "Come in."

"Hello." Kay tried very hard to keep the flatness from her voice. Expecting him to greet her in a pair of faded jeans and perhaps a sweater, or even shirtless, Kay stared at the tall, elegantly tailored man wearing a dark, expensive suit, a white shirt and a patterned tie of smooth silk. Shiny black Italian leather shoes looked as though they'd been freshly polished. Gold cuff links glittered at his wrists and his unruly, thick black hair was neatly brushed back off his dark face. He was, obviously, dressed to go out for the evening.

"I . . . I'll hurry," Kay offered lamely, feeling her cheeks splotching with crimson. "You must be in a hurry and . . ."

Sullivan smiled, took the empty suitcase from her hand and set it on the carpet, stepped behind her and took her coat. "No hurry," he said from above her ear. "I've a dinner engagement, but not for an hour."

"Good," she said, fighting the urge to fly at him and beat on the broad white-shirted chest. How she longed to reach up and muss all that thick black hair, to jerk the perfect knot from his silk tie, to shout at him that he could not go out looking so devastatingly handsome, that she simply would not allow it. "I'll not be long," she assured him and started down the hall to his bedroom.

"You know where everything is," he said politely and made no move to follow her.

Kay was glad. She was terrified that he'd see the shaking of her hands as she went about packing up her things. She needn't have worried. She stepped into his big bedroom and saw that all of her clothes had been neatly stacked on his bed, ready to be packed.

Three warm winter nightgowns that she'd never had on were the first items she saw. With a wince, she vividly re

alled that first night here when she'd drawn one of the soft,
eecy gowns from a bureau drawer and Sullivan had
aughed at her, snatched it from her hands and said teas-
igly, "In my bed, honey, you won't be needing this. I'll
eep you plenty warm."

Face flaming, Kay gathered the unused nighties, several
airs of lacy panties, a couple of sweaters and some bras
om the bed, shoving them all together with hurried, jerky
ovements.

"After I so carefully folded everything." Sullivan's deep
oice gently scolded from the doorway where he stood,
npty gray suitcase in his hand, leaning against the wooden
ame. He pushed away from the door, stepped forward and
laced the case on the bed, bending to unzip it and fold back
ie top.

Kay, wondering how long she could hold back her feel-
igs, said weakly, "I'm in a bit of a hurry. I'll straighten
verything out when I get home." She dumped everything
to the open suitcase while he stood, nodding. In seconds
verything that belonged to her had been stuffed haphaz-
dly into the bag, blouses and skirts and jeans still on their
angers. "That's it," she announced breathlessly.

She felt like screaming when he calmly said, "Not quite."

Into the bathroom he strode, returning with several
oothbrushes clutched in one hand. Kay gritted her teeth,
abbed them from him and jerked the loaded luggage from
s bed. Past him she flew, but easily he caught up to her.

"I'll carry it down to the car for you, Kay," he said, tak-
g the heavy case from her.

"That's not necessary." She heard the shrillness of her
oice, knew she was near losing all composure.

"I'll do it." He was adamant. "Get your coat."

Kay was in no mood to argue. They spoke not another
ord and when Sullivan had hoisted the heavy bag into the
unk of Kay's red car, Kay, already behind the wheel, didn't
other to say goodbye or thank you. She started the engine
id roared away, shooting a look up at the rearview mirror
see a tall, handsome man caught in the glow of her tail-

lights. His wide shoulders seemed to slump as he turned an
went back up the steps of the towering building.

Janelle Davis rubbed her temples. She pulled out h
middle desk drawer, looking for an aspirin. The consta
noise coming from the office next to hers was beginning t
wear on her nerves.

It was Wednesday afternoon. Sullivan had been f
riously chinning himself on the high steel rod off and o
since shortly after ten o'clock. This was the third consec
tive day of hearing him heave and blow and raise himse
repeatedly up to the bar. The third day of hearing him cras
to the floor, exhausted, only to return not ten minutes lat
for another prolonged session of strenuous chinning.

Janelle knew full well what was bothering him. Rumo
were rampant throughout the Denver radio communit
Sherry had wasted little time in spreading the word th
ABC in New York had called Kay Clark with a job offer i
mind. Janelle shook a couple of aspirins into her upturne
palm, shook her head and wished it were Kay Clark—n
the aspirin—that she was shaking.

A great crashing noise from next door preceded the soun
of Sullivan's office shower being turned on full blast. J
nelle rolled her eyes and wondered if this would be his la
shower of the day. She looked at the small leather-covere
clock on the corner of her desk. It was four o'clock. N
there'd be at least one more shower after this one if he we
home at his usual hour of six.

The week dragged for Kay. Yet it flew past much too fas
All week she'd clung to a thread of hope that Sullivan wou
turn to her behind the control panel and say, "Don't g
honey. Please stay with me." Or that he'd come to h
apartment. Or that he'd call her on the phone and tell h
that he wanted her back at his place where she belonged.

As the days passed and her trip to New York ap
proached, Kay began to sadly face the facts. He was n
going to stop her. He was going to let her fly up to Ne
York, be interviewed by ABC and accept should they off

r a job. She'd painted herself right into a corner and there
as no way she could get out.

It was Friday. The day she was to leave. The morning
ow went smoothly. Ten o'clock came quickly and after-
ard, Sullivan and Kay spent a couple of hours in the pro-
uction studio, cutting commercials for a shoe company.
he commercial spots were written by a clever copywriter.
hey were meant to be humorous and they were. So funny
ere the lines each was to say, Sullivan and Kay kept break-
g up and having to stop the tape and start over. A taping
at was supposed to take no longer than thirty minutes
retched into well over two hours.

Neither minded. They were having too much fun and for
time both forgot that on this very day, Kay would leave for
e big city. They were doing what they loved best with the
rson they loved doing it with and everything else was un-
portant.

Finally the commercial spots were completed, the laugh-
r had subsided and Kay, sliding down off the tall stool
here she'd been sitting next to Sullivan, looked at the clock
d said, "I've got packing to do, so I'll go."

"Oh, sure," Sullivan said easily, "run on along."

"Thanks," she said softly.

"Don't mention it." He turned to leave, but she laid a
nd on his arm. His dark head swung around and he faced
r.

Swallowing her pride, Kay looked up at the dear, hand-
me face and murmured ever so softly, "I'm going to-
ght, Sul, but until that plane takes off—" The rest was left
said. Tears were threatening to spill and she could no
nger trust her voice. Sullivan's eyes were as hard and cold
polished onyx. His tall, lean body was tensed and ungiv-
g.

Kay knew it was hopeless.

Sullivan's jaw tightened. "Good luck, Kay," he said,
rned away and hurried out of the production studios.

Her heart breaking, Kay followed him from the room and
ft the station.

Sullivan went directly to his office, closed the door a
walked to the chinning bar. Shortly after three in the afte
noon, after several sessions of his incessant chinning a
two showers, and with another headache starting behind h
eyes, Janelle Davis knocked on Sullivan's door.

Not waiting for an answer, she stepped inside, closed t
door and leaned back, her arms folded across her che
Sullivan, shirtless, perspiration glistening on his shoulde
and in his hair, lowered himself to the floor.

"She leaves on United's 7:00 p.m. flight for New York
Janelle looked straight into his eyes. Sullivan said nothin
"I checked," Janelle continued, "there's seats available
She smiled at the silent Sullivan, turned and left witho
another word.

Eleven

___

ay, looking cool and sophisticated in a well-tailored suit cream wool, brown silk blouse with its mandarin collar ted tightly around her long, elegant neck, silver hair aited into a thick coil and pinned atop her head, stepped o the first-class cabin of the New-York-bound jetliner.

Smiling absently to the stewardess who took her ticket, y located seat 3A and took the four steps down the aisle ward it, glancing around at the few passengers already ated. A middle-aged couple sat in the front two seats, the oman already reaching inside a big, floppy bag to pull out r knitting. Behind them, two tired-looking businessmen, e already dozing, held briefcases on their laps.

In the last row of seats, a pair of long legs encased in gray nnel slacks was crossed beneath a copy of the *Wall Street urnal*, which covered the face of its absorbed reader.

Kay took her window seat, buckled the belt tightly and ught the foolish fear already clawing at her stomach. artache was temporarily forgotten as passengers boarded, e front door was locked and Kay felt the movement of the

big plane beginning to taxi out toward the runway. Pal
perspiring, heart fluttering, Kay paid no attention to t
stewardess's canned speech.

Checking one last time to be certain that her seat belt w
as tight as she could get it, Kay licked dry lips and gripp
the armrests as the big jet turned onto the runway and s
felt the dreadful roar of the powerful engines drowning o
all other sound.

Eyes wide with fright, Kay looked out the tiny windo
her small body tensed, her fingers curling over the cha
arms in a death grip. Just as the heavy plane began to spe
ever faster down the runway, evenly spaced blue grou
lights sliding past the window so rapidly they were beco
ing a blur, Kay's head snapped around.

A lean brown hand gently covered a white-knuckled o
upon the armrest and Sullivan Ward buckled his seat b
with his other hand. Kay blinked at him in confusion th
changed almost immediately to relief.

"I seem to recall you being a little nervous on the tak
off." His deep, soothing voice had never sounded mo
wonderful to Kay. Sullivan plucked tight little fingers
from the chair arm, bringing her cold, stiff hand up to t
warmth of his sweatered chest. Both his hands closed ov
hers and when she swallowed and tried to speak, Sulliv
leaned close and said, smiling understandingly, "Darlin
wait until we're up, then we'll say it all." Dark eyes c
ressed her and he added, "You're safe, sweetheart. I'm h
with you. Everything will be fine."

A soft little gasp escaped Kay's parted lips. Blue ey
thanking him, Kay leaned her grateful head on his sho
der, took a deep breath and heard the captain saying fro
the cockpit, "On the climb out, you can see the lights of t
Mile High City twinkling up at you just as we skim the ve
peaks of the Rockies rising to a height of fourteen tho
sand feet above sea level."

Kay smiled. She made no move to look out her windo
at the lights the captain spoke of. She looked instead into t
shining dark eyes of the man clinging to her hand.

Sullivan was smiling down at her and Kay felt her fear of flying evaporate. If she remained a little short of breath, it no longer had anything to do with fear. It was pure, unexpected happiness.

"The captain has turned off the seat-belt signs," the voice over the intercom said, "you may now feel free to move around the cabin, but for your safety..."

Sullivan squeezed Kay's hand and said, "I suppose you'd like to know what I'm doing here."

Kay said honestly, "Yes, but whatever your reason, I'm glad you're here."

"You're sweet, and that will make it easier to say what I have on my mind." Sullivan nodded yes when the stewardess asked if they'd like a drink. "Champagne," he ordered for them both. Then he turned back to Kay and said, "Promise me that when you've heard me out, you'll give me a truly honest answer."

Brilliant blue eyes were wide. "I will," she told him and meant it.

"Kay, I love you. I want you to stay with me, but only if you're sure that you'd never regret it."

"Sul, the only thing I'd ever regret is losing you again. Don't you know that?"

"Then why are you at this moment bound for New York?"

"Because," she admitted, "I suppose I'm almost as stubborn as you."

"Kay, you're very sweet, but are you certain you don't really want the job in New York?" His eyes held a warmth and understanding she found achingly appealing. "I mean, believe it or not, darling, I love you enough that I want you to have—"

Kay interrupted. "Sul, you must believe me. I don't want the job in New York. I want nothing but to be your partner on the air in Denver."

"That's all you want? Sure?"

"Positive," she assured him.

"You don't think a year from now you'll wish you'd—"

"Never."

A broad grin lifted the corners of Sullivan's lips. "In that case, I've a suite reserved at the Hotel Pierre on the park. What would you say to a honeymoon in the Big Apple?"

Kay stared at him, speechless. Sullivan laughed and teased, "Does that mean yes or no, sweetheart?"

"Sul," she whispered breathlessly, "are you serious? How could we . . . I don't see how . . ."

"Kay, after this miserable week I knew I couldn't live without you; don't want to, refuse. That decided, I knew I'd have to swallow all my pride and come after you. Here I am, darling. I want you, I want to marry you this week in New York and spend a honeymoon with you at the Pierre. I told Sam Shults we needed a week off. He agreed. Now it's up to you."

"The answer is yes!"

Sullivan laughed. "You don't want to think about it for a day or two?"

"Sul, you've told me what you want; know what I want?"

"Tell me, sweet."

"I want to marry you just as soon as it is legally possible. I want us to spend an entire week inside that suite at the Pierre. I want to be on the morning show at Q102 in Denver with you as my partner for the next twenty years. I want to have your babies and—"

"Sweetheart—" Sullivan leaned closer "—would you be terribly embarrassed if I kissed you right now?"

Kay's answer was to turn parted lips up to his. Sullivan, his dark eyes filled with love, lowered his mouth to within one inch of hers and murmured, "Kiss me like there's no one else here."

"Is there?" she breathed and felt the sculpted male lips gently fit over hers. Kay's left hand came up from her lap to go behind his head and pull him closer. Her mouth opened beneath his and her tongue drew a heated line along his lips. Sullivan's mouth opened wider and his kiss deepened as he softly moaned.

Forgetting entirely where they were, Sullivan kissed her with rapidly increasing intensity and Kay clung to him and returned his ardor. The deep, drugging kiss was interrupted by the stewardess, clearing her throat just above them.

Sullivan reluctantly lifted his head, his black eyes still on the soft, parted lips he'd been kissing. Kay looked guiltily up at the red-faced stewardess and said, "I'm sorry, you see—"

"You see—" Sullivan grinned and accepted the stemmed glasses of champagne from the stewardess "—this woman has just agreed to become my bride and I felt that warranted a little kiss."

"I wholeheartedly agree." The stewardess nodded. "And may I offer congratulations." She flashed Kay a smile and made her way on down the aisle.

"Sul?"

"Hmm?"

"Will you kiss me again?" Kay took a sip of bubbly champagne.

"No, sorry." He lifted his glass to his lips.

"No?"

"You know what your sweet kisses do to me."

"Sul?"

"Yes?"

"Have you any idea how much I love you?"

"If it's half as much as I love you, I'm satisfied.

Kay's sleepy eyes slitted open. Disoriented, she looked out the tall window across from where she lay. Cold rain streaked down the panes. Kay slowly turned her head.

A handsome face was smiling warmly just above hers. Dark, sultry eyes were looking down at her. Sullivan pushed a shock of tangled hair back off her cheek and said in a low, warm voice, "My sweet, beautiful wife."

Kay lifted a slender hand to his jaw and started to speak. He stopped her. "Kay." Sullivan brushed his lips to hers. "I know you don't like to talk when you first waken. Doesn't matter. I love you and conversation is not what I want anynow."

Kay smiled at him and murmured, "Good morning, husband," and lifted her head for his kiss.

Sullivan shuddered. He pulled her bare body closer to the warmth of his and whispered huskily into her ear, "I had all kinds of things planned for today. You know, the museums and galleries and the Statue of Liberty, but damned if it's not raining." He began to nuzzle the softness just under her ear.

Kay sighed happily, wrapped her arms around his broad, bare back and closed her eyes. "I'm terribly disappointed. Think you can find some way to amuse me?"

Sullivan opened his lips and nibbled a path down the side of her warm, fragrant throat. "I'll need your help." His voice was growing heavy with desire.

"You have it, my love." She turned her face toward his.

Sullivan lifted his head, looked for a long, loving minute into his new bride's beautiful blue eyes, groaned and took her mouth with his. He kissed her passionately, devouringly, and Kay sighed into his mouth and felt her naked body being pressed closely to the long, lean body of her husband.

When finally Sullivan lifted his dark head, Kay looked into his eyes and said, "Promise me something, Sul."

"Anything," he murmured.

"You won't make me go see any museums or galleries or Broadway shows on this trip."

Heart hammering in his chest, Sullivan said happily, "Baby, that I promise." His mouth came back down on hers. Blood heated, hearts sped, bare bodies molded to each other.

Sullivan and Kay Ward, the hottest morning radio team of Denver, Colorado, enjoyed total anonymity in New York City. They could have gone wherever they chose and no one would have recognized or bothered them.

However, they took no chances. While cold winter rains drenched the huge, teeming city, the newlyweds stayed safely ensconced in their suite. Room service provided all meals.

Kay, who'd never before been to the city, smiled and stretched lazily in their big rumpled bed and had not the slightest curiosity about the sights spreading out below their top-floor suite. All she wanted was in this room with her.

Kay clasped her husband to her, bit his ear playfully and said, "You know something, Sul?"

"What?"

"Someday we'll have to come back to New York and look around."

"Yeah," he agreed, kissing her throat, "we'll have to do that."

READERS' COMMENTS ON SILHOUETTE DESIRES

"Thank you for Silhouette Desires. They are the best thing that has happened to the bookshelves in a long time."

—V.W.*, Knoxville, TN

"Silhouette Desires—wonderful, fantastic—the best romance around."

—H.T.*, Margate, N.J.

"As a writer as well as a reader of romantic fiction, I found DESIREs most refreshingly realistic—and definitely as magical as the love captured on their pages."

—C.M.*, Silver Lake, N.Y.

"I just wanted to let you know how very much I enjoy your Silhouette Desire books. I read other romances, and I must say your books rate up at the top of the list."

—C.N.*, Anaheim, CA

"Desires are number one. I especially enjoy the endings because they just don't leave you with a kiss or embrace; they finish the story. Thank you for giving me such reading pleasure."

—M.S.*, Sandford, FL

*names available on request